PRAISE FOR

MIDNIGHT IN CRYSTAL CITY

"*Midnight in Crystal City* was riveting and had a very good storyline, so I wanted to see how it ended. I came to care about the characters and was happy with the way the pieces fit together. I would recommend it highly to anyone wanting a pleasant read. It pulls you in quickly such that you can visualize the characters and want to see how they develop throughout the story."

—Tom Freeman

"I thoroughly enjoyed [*Midnight in Crystal City*]. I thought it flowed well and it was an easy and enjoyable read. The story was intriguing.

"I liked how the focus was on Michael and his relationship with his daughter. As that relationship progressed in the story, many other issues in Michael's life played out. His relationship with his job, Donna, and the other characters made the journey through the book interesting. I particularly liked the way all the events impacting Michael's life came together and brought the story to a close. As he said at the end of the book, 'There is a God. There is a meaning to life.' . . .

"I hope many others will read the book. I think they will enjoy it as much as I did."

—Marty Muscatello

Midnight In Crystal City
by R. R. Beach

© Copyright 2025 R. R. Beach

ISBN 979-8-88824-652-8

All rights reserved. No part of this publication may be reproduced, stored in a retrieval system, or transmitted in any form or by any means—electronic, mechanical, photocopy, recording, or any other—except for brief quotations in printed reviews, without the prior written permission of the author.

This is a work of fiction. All the characters in this book are fictitious, and any resemblance to actual persons, living or dead, is purely coincidental. The names, incidents, dialogue, and opinions expressed are products of the author's imagination and are not to be construed as real.

Published by

3705 Shore Drive
Virginia Beach, VA 23455
800-435-4811
www.koehlerbooks.com

MIDNIGHT IN CRYSTAL CITY

R. R. BEACH

VIRGINIA BEACH
CAPE CHARLES

HELEN

It's midnight in Crystal City. I seldom dream, but when I do, it's always the same. It's always about Helen. This time, I'm running through a moonlit forest, darting among huge boulders left over from some long-ago ice age. It's windy, and the treetops are swaying back and forth in a rhythmic dance. I spot her among the boulders, her dark hair wild from the wind. She's calling, laughing. It's the laugh she had before the drinking and the fighting, before it became bitter and mocking. In the moonlight, our eyes meet. Now I'm running after her, calling out as her dark shadow flits among the trees, in and out of the boulders. Then, suddenly, there's no more forest, no more boulders. Too late, I realize I've fallen off a rocky outcropping. Beneath me, there's nothing but a sea of fog.

I flail at the hotel sheets, trying to wake up, my mouth frozen in a silent scream, T-shirt drenched in a cold sweat. At last, I'm fully awake, staring at the blank wall of the hotel room. I stumble out of bed, find my way to the window, and open the curtains. Before me is a nightscape of empty boulevards and now vacant office buildings.

I want to call Holly, but it's way too late. And she would only hang up. *She can't hate me forever*, I tell myself. But I don't believe it.

I'm restless and can't go back to sleep. I put on jeans and some sneakers, grab the keycard, and head out. In the hotel lobby, I nod to the clerk who gives me a disgusted look, like I'm going out to find some action, a hooker or something.

Outside, the air is stale and lifeless, except for steam venting from unseen pipes. There is no movement anywhere. Off in the distance, a traffic light changes from red to green, but all the cars have long since headed home to the suburbs.

To be in motion, that's all that matters. I put the dream of Helen out of my mind and walk aimlessly past the entrance to the underground mall, all closed up and locked. A security guard looks out from behind glass doors, foggy from condensation. I hardly notice.

Planes are still landing at the airport on the other side of the railroad tracks. But I've been staying at the hotel for several days, and the sound of jets reversing their engines is now merely white noise.

Finally, I stop and look about. Without realizing it, I made my way onto the pedestrian overpass to the airport. I can look up and down the main highway for many blocks. Still nothing. Just streetlights and a canyon of office buildings. A breeze kicks up. Voices come from somewhere on the other side of the pedestrian overpass. I make my way over to investigate. There's a kiosk with an industrial-grade TV protected by thick plexiglass. It's locked, and only some unknown municipal worker has the key. There must be a speaker mounted nearby because I can hear the sound clearly.

"There are no accidents," comes a voice from the speakers. "Consciously or subconsciously, our actions fulfill the histories that have been preordained for us."

It's a late-night talk show. The guest is going on about the theme of his latest book, which the host holds up so that the camera can get a close-up.

"What about wars and natural disasters?" the host asks. "What about the holocaust?"

Yeah, what about all that stuff? What about wives with drinking problems? What about little girls who grow up with no mommy? How the hell do you preordain that?

"Those individuals allowed themselves to become victims," says the guest. "That was the history they chose for themselves."

"All six million of them?" the host asks, trying to filter the disbelief in his voice since his job is to help his guests sell their books.

I get fidgety. Wanting to turn off the TV but realizing I can't, I scan the street for a rock or piece of debris to heave through the plexiglass. From out of nowhere, there's a tap on my shoulder. I freeze. Sure I'm about to get mugged or worse.

I turn to face a huge man in tattered rags. He's homeless. He points at the TV. "What bullshit," he says. "Like we got any fucking choice in what happens to us. Like I had any choice in what Blue Ties did to me."

I want to run, but the huge man has cut off any means of escape. My only option is to hop the handrail to the street below, at least twenty feet down.

"What's your name, buddy?"

"Michael," I tell him.

"Mine's Ben."

"You got a cigarette, Michael?"

"Don't smoke," I say as casually as I can, still looking for an escape route. "Who's Blue Ties?" I ask. Not that I really care. It's a diversionary tactic. This guy seems a little off, like the elevator doesn't go all the way to the top floor.

Ben lets loose an unearthly laugh. "Only the most evil man in the universe. Destroyed my life. Turned me into a freak with his steroids and mind control. He made me do the bad things. But I never killed no one. No, I never did that."

Another jet lands, engines reversing. I look at the huge man's face. It's mottled and smeared with the grime of living on the streets for too many years. The face is looking out beyond me, momentarily frozen. The sound of the jet dies out.

The face comes to life again. "Hey, you got any money?"

Digging through my pockets, I find a five-dollar bill and hand it to him, not sure whether I'm being mugged or not. He tucks it somewhere deep inside his clothing. While he's distracted with this, I see an opening and turn to walk away. A huge hand grabs me by the shoulder and spins me around. I brace myself for a blow.

"If you see Blue Ties," Ben says, "let me know. I'll have to get out of town. Or hurt somebody."

"You don't like this Blue Ties fellow, do you?"

"Would you? If he ruined your life?" Ben takes the end of a purple scarf draped about his neck and sniffs it. "Shannon and I were going to get married. Blue Ties ruined that."

There's the sound of a trash can being knocked over somewhere off in the distance. Probably just a tomcat, but Ben freezes. "Gotta go," he says nervously, then hurries off into the night.

I'm left alone on the pedestrian overpass. Over at the airport, a jet is revving its engines, preparing for takeoff. I think about the poor bastards on the plane, no doubt hours behind schedule.

UNCIVIL SERVANTS

THE CONFERENCE TABLE IS WELL POLISHED, long and sleek, nicely dimensioned. Its grainy wood is highlighted by pale-yellow light filtering through windows, gray from the accumulated grit of the city. I slide my hand across the table, entranced by its beauty, pondering the inconsistency of its existence amidst this sea of turgid federal gray.

It was a good presentation, I tell myself. Good enough anyway. To the point, yet simple enough that even the likes of Kloucek could understand. I laugh to myself at the title on the first slide: A Decision Support Tool for Strategic Decision Making. Was it Kloucek or Markowitz that came up with that? I laugh because that's just what the government needs: more software. It's all meant to give the illusion of doing something so that resumes can get beefed up and people can get promoted, but without really changing anything.

I catch a glimpse of Donna's reflection in the conference table. I look up. She smiles. For a moment, I feel she can see through me, to the empty man inside. I want to say something smart, a witty wisecrack about Kloucek or Markowitz or the whole decaying system, just to reassure myself that I'm not completely dead inside. But Kloucek is in the middle of wrapping things up, and it would be inappropriate. So I just smile a smile that says, *It's the same old same old.*

Kloucek goes on about everyone getting on the same page and pulling together and all that bullshit. The heads of Markowitz and his minions bob up and down in agreement. Markowitz even says, "Exactly, Ron. That's spot on."

Inevitably, my mind drifts off to other things. Holly's little again, standing in an inflatable pool; I'm taking pictures while she hams it up for the camera. She slips and falls on her bottom, starts to cry, remembers the camera, and giggles. We giggle together.

Kloucek clears his throat. "Frankly, Michael," he says, "I'm very disappointed." I snap out of my daydreaming, place my hands on the conference table, and pretend to be interested, to be professional. I smile at Markowitz, at the minions. But I've dealt with Kloucek before and know he likes to hear himself talk. I try to look concerned.

"Sorry to hear that, Ron," I tell him, not sure where he's going with this.

Kloucek looks at Donna. "You see what I'm saying. Don't you?" She looks at him blankly. "You know, the agency motto: Let's be great together." Donna still looks back blankly. Kloucek's speech slows, like he's speaking to children. "The Decision Support Tool doesn't solve our resource allocation problem. Who stays; who goes. Get it?"

Now I do. "You mean the optimization module?" I ask in disbelief. "That was thoroughly discussed up and down the chain of command. I thought everyone agreed to hold off until the basic concept was proven."

Kloucek shakes his head violently. "No, no, no, we need to come out firing more than blanks. We need to hit a home run." Kloucek looks at Donna, at me, then says, "There's been a basic communication failure on this. Again, let's be great together."

I'm speechless. The contract's been signed for months. There's not one dime for an optimization module. My eyes plead with Donna to talk some sense into Kloucek.

Everyone follows Kloucek out into the hallway. Kloucek and Markowitz immediately huddle together near a big window.

They have an animated chat, and then, almost simultaneously, both pull out their cell phones. I'm willing to bet there is no one on the other end of Kloucek's. He's not above posturing just to look good in front of Markowitz.

The minions cluster together further down the hall. They've all pulled out their cell phones too and have serious looks pasted on their faces.

I start to ask Donna what Kloucek's been smoking but think better of it. There's silence as everyone finishes up with the cell phones, except for Markowitz down the hallway still mumbling into his. In slow motion, his lone, hollow voice bounces off the walls. Somewhere deep within the bowels of the building an air handler kicks in. I swear I can hear the whole bureaucratic mechanism grinding slowly away. Like a huge, beached whale dying a slow death.

Donna comes over. "How was your trip up here?"

"Okay," I tell her. "Except 66 was a parking lot."

"It gets worse every day. How about your hotel?"

"Okay. I find the sound of 737s taking off every five minutes very restful. Actually, I couldn't sleep for some reason."

"The planes?"

"No. I'm used to that. Just restless."

I'm about to describe my encounter with Ben when Kloucek summons Donna. "My master calls," she says and scurries over to talk to him.

I have a moment to myself, so I pull my cell phone from my trousers and enter Holly's phone number, sure that she's screening my calls. I'm about to hang up before her voicemail kicks in when a voice comes on the phone, "This is Holly."

"Holly?" I'm still not sure if it's Holly or her voicemail.

"Yes." There's now a note of impatience. "Michael? Is that you? I've told you not to call me."

"Please, Holly," I beg. "It's been years. Why can't we just talk? Or come by? I'm here in Crystal City."

"You know why."

Then there's a dial tone.

I realize it was a mistake to call her. I'm left standing in the hall, the cell phone dangling from my arm. Memories of the night Helen died racing through my head.

"You all right?" comes a voice. It's Donna. "We must be working you too hard," she jokes. "You checked out for a minute." She takes my empty hand and shakes it. It occurs to me that we've never touched before, despite months and months of meetings, working lunches, technical discussions.

"My daughter," I tell her. "We're . . . estranged."

"Sorry to hear that," she says. She gives my hand one last squeeze. We head back into the conference room and sit down.

"Where's Kloucek and Markowitz?" I ask.

"They had to scurry off to the secretary's office. They want us to scope out the requirements for the optimization module so they can decide which features they want."

"That'll take weeks."

"Sorry. I guess we're stuck with each other for a while."

I can think of worse fates. I'm scheduled to return to the office tomorrow. But the truth is there's nothing there for me anymore. Too many bridges burned and all that. There are coworkers, but all my close friends have moved on to other jobs. It's surprising to realize I'd rather stay in Crystal City. I'm close to Holly, even though she won't talk to me. And there's my younger brother, Jimmy. There's always Jimmy. He was there when it happened, when Helen died.

I turn to Donna and smile. "The problem is," I tell her, "our systems people needed to be working on this weeks ago to meet your timeline. I'll need to call Jonathan. We'll need another contract."

"Okay," Donna says. "I'll get our people on it."

"Okay. I still don't understand what happened," I tell her. "It wasn't our idea to leave the optimization module out. Jonathan and I thought it was a necessary part of the system. In fact, as I recall, it was Kloucek who thought it was overkill. All but accused us of profiteering."

"He misread Markowitz," she says. "Thought it was all a big show for the secretary. You know, a lot of smoke and mirrors, but no real change in anything. Turns out Markowitz and the secretary have to do something. We're facing big cuts in our funding. The secretary has to have a transition plan that he can defend."

I mull this over. "How can you stand working in this bureaucratic labyrinth?" I laugh.

Donna chuckles too. She's about to say something when the door to the conference room slowly opens. A strange, pock-faced man walks in. He's wearing a rumpled white shirt, partially unbuttoned. There's a nervous expression on Donna's face. She nods to the man and looks down as she shuffles some papers.

"Hi, sweetheart," the man says. He's working a toothpick as he says it. He makes his way to a chair at the end of the conference table. He pulls out a newspaper and makes a big display of spreading it out to read.

Donna is clearly intimidated. I get up to go over and say something. Point out that there's a meeting in progress or something. But Donna leans over and tugs on my sleeve. She makes an odd facial expression that says, *please sit down*. I ease back into my chair, all the while eyeing the pock-faced man.

The three of us sit there in silence. Minute after minute ticks by with only the sound of newspaper pages turning. Without warning, the pock-faced man abruptly gets up and folds the newspaper under his arm. "See ya toots," he says, looking directly at Donna, and then walks out.

"Who the hell was that?" I finally ask.

"Cronin," she says very softly. "He really gives me the creeps."

"He can't treat you like that," I say indignantly. "Isn't it harassment or something?"

Donna fiddles with some papers in front of her but says nothing.

"Why don't you say something to Kloucek?"

"I have. He laughed. He said, 'Take on Cronin? You got to be kidding.'"

"And did nothing?"

"Nothing changed. But I checked around. Turns out Cronin used to be with some super-secret spy agency, a so-called black-funded agency, before coming to us. No one knows if he's still a spy or was just put out to pasture."

"You don't mind if I say something to him, do you? I can be very persuasive."

Donna's face visibly pales. "Oh, Michael . . . Please don't. They say he's still very dangerous."

COLD WAR 1

THE AIR IS STILL. It's midmorning in Crystal City. No smokers huddled in doorways. No one out taking an extended coffee break. The homeless have long since retreated into the shadows and crevices of the urban landscape. The only human about at this one moment in time is a young man on the pedestrian overpass, a skateboarder. He's wearing baggy pants that barely stay up and high-priced basketball shoes with laces untied. On his head, a ball cap points backward. On his right forearm, a tattoo of two red interlocking circles.

He hears something on the other side of the overpass. He throws down his skateboard and rolls over to check it out. In one fluid motion, he pulls up and launches the skateboard into the air with his foot. Then casually plucks it out of midair and folds it under his arm.

"It's a fucking TV," he says out loud, although there is no one around to hear. "What's it doing here?"

He hits the Plexiglas case with his fist. Nothing happens. He holds his sore hand. He finds a broken chunk of concrete and heaves it as hard as he can at the TV. It bounces harmlessly away. He stands hypnotized before the wonder of the hardened TV. There's a BBC documentary on. Russian frigates are plowing their way through the choppy seas of the Atlantic. The camera zooms in on what are obviously missiles on the deck of one of the frigates. In a clipped BBC accent, the narrator says, "More than any other episode, the Cuban Missile Crisis defined the Kennedy administration, whose image suffered from the Bay of Pigs fiasco. Oddly enough, it also marked the beginning of the end for Khrushchev."

Cuba, the skateboarder thinks, *where cigars come from?*

There are now pictures of US warships aggressively making their way through heavy seas to intercept the Russian frigates. Then Navy fighter planes swooping low over the Russian ships.

The images fade out, and there's a commercial break. A beautiful, seductive woman in a low-cut gown comes on the screen and blows a kiss to the viewers, then gives a bashful look over her shoulder. It's a commercial for men's cologne, *Envy*. A banner at the bottom of the screen asks: Are you man enough?

"Envy this!" the skateboarder says out loud and grabs his crotch. There's still no one around to hear him.

NIGHT AIR

I'M CHASING HELEN OVER A RAILROAD TRESTLE. She's on a flat car, pumping like crazy, up and down, up and down. I'm on foot, trying not to look down between the crossties at the surging river below. Now she's on the other side, all spent, collapsed over the hand pump. I can easily catch up with her. But there's a cry from the other embankment. It's the cry of a little girl. "Daddy, wait for me." It must be Holly. There's the rumble of a train approaching, coming around the last bend before the trestle, its whistle blowing louder and louder. What to do? Catch up with Helen and finally say the words that make everything right with her or save Holly from the train?

I wake up, eyes wide open, looking straight up at the ceiling. I realize I'm still staying at the same Crystal City hotel. Even though it's past midnight, I want to call Holly but think better of it and call Jimmy instead.

"Who's this?" Jimmy answers, obviously offended that anyone would call so late.

"It's me."

"Do you have any life at all?" he asks, half pissed, half joking.

"I had a dream about Helen. Holly was in it too. I woke up and needed to call her."

"It's too damn late to be calling anyone. You know how I feel about this. Tell her the truth. She thinks you were responsible for her mom's death. Tell her what really happened."

"I can't. She would hate me more for ruining the memory of her mom. And for lying about it all these years."

"You should have told her what really happened. Years ago, you should have told her. I can understand protecting a little girl from the truth about her mom, but now you owe her the truth."

"You're right, but now . . . Now it's too late. It would devastate her. I can't be responsible for that."

"Sooner or later, the truth has to be told. I was there, remember. I know it wasn't your fault."

"Yeah. Well, I'm not so sure about that."

"Trust me," Jimmy says, "It'll work out."

I say goodbye. Tell Jimmy I'm sorry I called so late. But I'm still restless. I grab the key card to the room and head out. I walk briskly along the sidewalk, a lone man in an empty cityscape. My mind churns through the last twenty-five years of my life. How in the world did things reach the point where the most important person in my life refuses to talk to me? How did things with Helen ever reach the point they did that fateful night?

Then there's Jimmy. Our lives have always been entwined. I remember a trip to the beach when we were young, wrestling in the salt water of the bay until our mom made us come out, eyes burning from the salt, fingers shriveled like prunes. Then eating peanut butter and banana sandwiches on the beach, Jimmy's favorite. Now, we'll probably both go to our graves with the secret of Helen's death.

It occurs to me there was something in Jimmy's voice at the end of our conversation, a tone he always has just when he was about to do something different or daring. *Keep out of this, Jimmy*, I think. *You'll just make things worse.*

In the middle of all these thoughts, there's the sudden image of the strange man that sat in on the meeting with Donna. Cronin? Was that his name? What a creep.

At last, I can take no more. I pull up. Take a deep breath of night air. I find myself on the pedestrian overpass again. The hardened TV is still playing on the other side. Do they ever turn that thing off?

"Got a cigarette?" Startled, I spin about. Before me stands the huge homeless man from before.

"What are you doing here?" I ask. Then remember his name, "Ben."

"Didn't mean to scare you," Ben says. "Got a cigarette? That's right, you don't smoke. I remember now. I didn't either back when I was competing."

I mechanically unroll a five-dollar bill and hand it to Ben, who immediately tucks it into some hidden fold of his clothing. But tonight, Ben seems more interested in talking than taking a handout.

"I loved football," Ben says. "I was a tight end. Wanted to play running back, but Coach made me play tight end because of my size. In the spring, I threw discus for the track team."

Ben's talking, but his eyes are a million miles away. He pauses. Looks at me. "You ever play football?"

"Marching band. Trumpet," I answer.

"Me too," Ben's smiling. For a moment, I forget he's a homeless man. "Except I played tuba." Ben places a big paw of a hand on my shoulder. I freeze, not sure what comes next. But there are tears welling up in his eyes. "I loved playing tuba, even more than football. I was All-State in both and state champ in discus."

"No kidding. I bet your mom and dad were proud."

"I guess, but I can barely remember them. Once Blue Ties and Dr. Seagrove got through with me, I could barely remember my own name."

"Who are they?"

"Just the two evilest men ever. They're the ones that ruined my football career."

Ben is beginning to sound like a homeless man again. It's very late now, and I start to wish I was back in the hotel room, sleeping between the crisp white sheets of my bed.

Ben's speech becomes more animated. "If I ever see either one of them again, I'll kill them with my bare hands. Back then, back when they turned me into a zombie with Dr. Seagrove's injections and their mind control tricks, I couldn't do anything about it. But now I'm free of all that, I could easily kill either one, especially Blue Ties, especially him. He was the one in charge."

I fight the urge to try and duck under Ben and flee to the safety of my hotel room. Instead, I try to humor him.

"You don't really want to kill anybody, do you?" I ask.

"Wouldn't you? If they had ruined your life? I was happy with football and playing the tuba. I once caught three touchdown passes against Eastside and played my tuba in the marching band at halftime. Blue Ties stole me away from all of that for his own dirty schemes."

"What do you mean?"

"He literally stole me away. Made me do things I didn't want to do. He saw me playing football, saw how big and strong I was, and used me for his own dirty, evil schemes."

"Surely, your parents would've stopped him."

"That's how sick they were. My parents never knew. They drugged me up one day after practice, one of Dr. Seagrove's 'special cocktails,' they called it. They drove me to a motel room. There were women there. Dr. Seagrove's wife and some of her friends. They were all dressed up in cocktail dresses and high heels. They kept teasing me, telling me what a big, handsome guy I was. Mrs. Seagrove came over and started stroking my business."

"You're business?"

"Yeah, you know. My privates."

"Oh. Right."

"Normally, I would've told them all to go to hell. But I was too drugged up. It was like a fog. I remembered them ladies teasing me and dragging me into the back room. I don't remember what happened next, but Dr. Seagrove was there too because he had pictures the next day. Of me lying in bed with each of the women. The sick bastard."

For a moment, time is frozen. Ben's mind seems to have whirred to a halt. Far off down the avenue, the headlights of a lone car slowly plow through the night.

Ben finally sighs. "I had to go along with them; they would have showed my mom them pictures. That would have killed her. I had to go along with their crazy plot."

"What crazy plot?" I'm compelled to ask.

"The plot to kill that Russian. Damn if I can ever remember his name. All those Russian names sound alike to me."

I've had enough. I'm ready to head back to the hotel room. I'm sure Ben is harmless and would not physically stop me—at least not this night. I'm about to make up some excuse to leave when I'm blinded by a spotlight. There's a disembodied voice. "Place your hands above your head! Don't move."

"Gotta go," Ben whispers. "Might be Blue Ties' people." As he starts to slip off into the shadows, he pauses. Giggling to himself, "Gorbachev. That was that Russian's name. Funny how, after all of these years, I can still remember." Then he disappears into the darkness.

A few moments later a cop is standing on the pedestrian overpass. "Hands over your head," he shouts. His service revolver is drawn. "There were two of you. Where's the other guy."

"I don't know," I tell him. It's the truth. *Where has Ben gone?* I wonder.

"Where does he live?"

"He's homeless."

"What are you doing out this late?" the officer asks, his service revolver still drawn. "You saying you two just bumped into each other?"

"I couldn't sleep. Had to get out of the hotel room. I guess he thought he could bum a cigarette. Is that gun loaded?"

"You let me worry about the gun." The cop reappraises the situation, decides I look too clueless to be a drug dealer, and holsters the gun. "Well, if I were you, I wouldn't get too friendly with the natives. Could be bad for your health, if you get my drift." He motions me to move on with a shrug of his shoulders, laughing at his own joke. "Yeah, could be bad for your health."

UNCLE JIMMY

IT'S EVENING RUSH HOUR ON THE INNER LOOP. Jimmy sits in his car, inching along. It's dinged and scratched and has a big dent in the front quarter panel, scars from years of commuting. Long ago he learned it didn't pay to invest in new vehicles. There was always someone following too close or cutting you off. Trading paint was just part of the commuting experience as far as he was concerned.

All around drivers are honking, shouting, flipping each other off. But he hardly notices. It's white noise. His mind is fixed on the tragedy of Michael's life. *I was there*, he thinks. *I know what happened. Holly's blaming the wrong person. But what else can she do? Michael refuses to tell her what really happened. Misguided. Senseless. No one can do anything.*

Jimmy is literally nudged out of his thoughts. The car behind has tapped his rear bumper. He looks up, startled. Space has opened up in front of him and the car behind is impatient to get moving. Jimmy rolls down the car window and mechanically flips him off. There's an instant response with the car horn. He accelerates to fill the gap and, within moments, is inching along the inner loop again. The driver behind is still insanely honking his horn. *He taps me again*, Jimmy thinks, *he's going to get a briefcase through his windshield.* The honking finally stops. Traffic comes to a dead stop. No one is moving.

On an impulse, Jimmy picks up his cell phone and dials Holly's number. She should be home by now since her condo is only a few blocks from a Metro stop.

"Hello," comes Holly's voice on the other end.

"Hi. It's Uncle Jimmy. I'm stuck on the inner loop in traffic and thought I would give you a call."

"How are you?" she says. She seems friendly enough, but Jimmy detects a weariness in her voice. "What do you want?" she adds.

"Do I need a reason to give my favorite niece a call?"

"Is this about Michael?"

Jimmy can sense the irritation in her voice. Odd that she refers to her dad by his first name. "Here's a thought," he says. "Why don't you let your Uncle Jimmy take you out to dinner? To that new little microbrewery in Shirlington."

"Sorry. I just don't think I can. The library has been really busy. We just got a whole new collection of primitive art donated. It's going to take weeks just to sort and classify it."

"You know I'm not going to buy that. Don't make me bring out the big guns. That I'm your only uncle. The only family you got around here."

Holly's tone softens. "Uncle Jimmy, it's nothing against you. It's just Michael. I don't want to talk about all that, what he did."

"I promise we won't talk about any of that," Jimmy says. He knows he's lying. "It's just been too long. We're family."

"Okay. But one word of Michael and I'm out of there."

"Great. About seven? Capital City Brewery, I think they call it."

"I know where it is," she says and hangs up.

By now the traffic has crawled through the last bottleneck. There's nothing but raw interstate for three counties. Like wild horses penned up for too long, cars zip in and out of traffic. A low-slung, souped-up black Honda cuts Jimmy off, the passenger looking directly at Jimmy and yelling obscenities at him through the window. But Jimmy's lost in thought. His mind has drifted back in time to the night Holly's mom died.

CAPITAL CITY

THE NEXT NIGHT FINDS JIMMY SITTING in a booth at the microbrewery waiting for Holly. He nibbles on a fresh, hot pretzel, the signature appetizer on the menu. He's getting cold feet, thinking maybe they'll just have a nice little dinner, chat about old times, not bring up the one episode that has defined Holly's life, all their lives, for the last twenty years. But his resolve returns. *She's got to know the truth*, he tells himself. *It's got to be better than that stupid lie we concocted that horrible night so long ago.*

He sees a reflection in the mirror behind the bar. Holly's entering through the glass doors of the restaurant. Jimmy turns and waves as she makes her way over to the booth. She takes off her coat and slides it next to her on the cushioned seat. She smiles at Jimmy. *Maybe Michael's right*, he thinks. She's better off not knowing the truth about her mom. But now there's no turning back. The truth is an expressway with no exit ramp.

"They got great soft pretzels here," he says as he signals the waitress over. "More pretzels here," he tells her. Turning to Holly, he asks how she's doing. Tells her about the horrible traffic from the night before. That it gets worse every day.

"That's why I prefer my little condo in the city," Holly says. "It's not much, but at least I don't spend half my life sitting in a car."

They go through the pretzels. Both remark on how warm and doughy they are. Holly orders a salad and an iced tea, and Jimmy orders meatloaf and a pale ale. As they dine, they discuss the past, carefully steering away from any discussion of Michael. Jimmy fights back a tear as he remembers Holly babysitting his daughter, Hanna, who is now married with twin girls and too busy to visit. They both remember Jimmy's wife, Debra, now dead of breast cancer ten years. Holly tells him that she was the closest thing she had to a mom growing up, and she still makes the lasagna recipe that Aunt Debra taught her.

"Do you have a boyfriend?" Jimmy asks.

"No. Don't have time for one."

"No men in your life?"

"Just Ian, a guy I work with."

"I envy you guys," Jimmy says, "Working in the Library of Congress sounds so interesting."

"Actually, it's pretty boring stuff for the most part. Cataloging, a little bit of research."

"Is it true they found George Washington's teeth in a cardboard box in the basement?"

For the first time since she came into the microbrewery, she laughs. "That's just an urban myth," she says. "Nothing to it. But occasionally, you do come across some really interesting stuff."

"Like what?"

"Sigmund Freud's vial of cocaine. Charles Dickens' walking cane. Ike's notes to his mistress."

"Ike had a mistress?"

"Evidently it was common knowledge at the time."

Jimmy shakes his head. "Another icon destroyed. Anything else. Any really juicy stuff, like what's really buried beneath the Sphinx?"

"Every once in a while, we come across some really confidential stuff. Unbelievable stuff."

"Like what?"

"Like Nixon was contemplating declaring martial law during Watergate, just to keep the reporters at bay."

"But how does something like that end up in the Library of Congress? You'd think Nixon would have destroyed it before it came back to bite him in the ass."

"People donate reams of stuff every day. Memos, letters, position papers. Seldom do they bother going through it to make sure there's nothing incriminating. I think the assumption is it will stay buried in some storage room somewhere. They don't realize we have to classify and review everything that comes through the door."

They finish their dinners. The waitress comes and takes their plates and brings back the check. Holly offers to at least pay for her dinner, but Jimmy insists it's his treat. She starts to gather up her things and thanks him for dinner, saying she enjoyed it.

Jimmy peers over his glasses. He hesitates. "There's something I need to tell you," he says.

"You're scaring me," Holly says. "Are you okay? I mean health-wise."

"It's about your dad."

Jimmy can see the anger growing in Holly's eyes.

"That's off limits, and you know it," she says. "I thought I could trust you to at least keep your word." She grabs her purse and coat and starts sliding out of the booth. Jimmy is still looking down at the check.

"Your dad wasn't driving the car that night," he says quietly.

Holly stops, motionless. "Are you insane?" Now she's really angry. Angry to the point of crying, her voice rises, and people around them have stopped eating, wondering what is going on.

"Please hear me out," Jimmy all but whispers. "Your dad wasn't driving the car the night your mom died. I was there. I know the truth."

"But I've got a dozen newspaper clippings that say otherwise. You are really out of line, Uncle Jimmy."

Now it seems like the whole restaurant is frozen.

"It's time for the truth to be told," Uncle Jimmy says. He chuckles sadly. "It couldn't make things any worse than they already are. Your dad loves you. More than you can ever imagine."

"I can never forgive him for what he did," she says, sliding back into the booth. "He was driving, lost control, and my mother died because of it. Like I said, I have the newspaper clippings to prove it. On top of that, when I confronted him, he admitted that he'd been drinking."

"You can't believe everything you read in the newspapers," Jimmy says half-jokingly. "I know what really happened."

"It's time for me to go. I've got a cat to feed." She's all set to get up and walk out of the restaurant, but she hesitates. Maybe from a need to know what her uncle would say. Maybe from just a moment of fatigue from the constant stream of activity that comes from urban living.

Jimmy seizes the opportunity to continue. "Look, your mom and dad loved each other. They really did, but life is never that simple. They would have huge fights. She felt hemmed in by family life, lack of money. He hated her drinking. But things were getting better. I truly believe if it wasn't for that night, that party, they would've worked things out eventually."

"You mean the party mentioned in all the newspaper accounts I found in our attic? The Hackenworths' party?"

"Everyone was there. Your mom and dad. Your Aunt Debra and me. All our friends."

"Right. And Michael drank too much, drove when he shouldn't have, and my mom died. End of story." Holly is about to leave again.

"Please hear me out. That's what your dad wanted the police to believe. We made it look that way. Your mom started drinking, started accusing your dad of unthinkable things, all lies. She grabbed the keys to the car and left the party. It was a horrible night, wind and rain everywhere. We went after her and found her on the parkway, wrapped around an oak tree. Her hair matted with blood. She groaned, came to for just a moment. She looked at your dad and brushed his face with the back of her hand. Then she was gone. We were both crying. But your dad gathered himself. 'This will never do,' he told me. So we made it look like your dad was driving. 'Holly can't know her mother had a drinking problem,' he said. That was it. He wanted to protect you. And it worked. Actually, it worked too good. You had to go nosing around the attic and come across those old newspapers."

Jimmy can tell by Holly's furrowed brow that she's agitated. He braces himself; he's not sure for what.

"So it's my fault?" she hisses. "You're blaming a little girl for wanting to find out the truth about her life?"

"No. No. Of course not. I just want you to understand that all your dad has ever wanted to do is protect you. To protect the memory of your mother. The plan was to tell you she was sick, had gone to live with the angels, until you were old enough. Then your dad was going to tell you what really happened. Of course, it wasn't what really happened. Not even close. It was what we made up in those few minutes before the police arrived. But you found the clippings first and immediately assumed your dad was hiding the truth from you."

Holly gathers up her handbag. She gets her car keys out of her jacket, slides out of the booth, stands up, and looks down at Jimmy.

"So he lies to me for twenty years," she says. "That's worse. Much worse."

She spins on her heels and storms out of Capital City. As she leaves, Jimmy watches her reflection in the big mirror behind the bar, along with the headlights of passing cars and people passing by outside.

CRONIN

I'M SITTING IN THE CONFERENCE ROOM, looking out the window, watching the sun as it sets behind an endless forest of government office buildings. Donna is at the front of the conference table updating Kloucek on the status of the Decision Support Tool. There's a progress chart projected on the screen behind her. But I pay little attention to it. I follow a rogue tendril of sunlight to Donna's foot. She's wearing high heels, red and open-toed.

Donna is wrapping it up. "The proposed enhancements will provide the cross-leveling capability we've needed for some time. It will provide a more equitable distribution of human resources among all our regions."

It's standard government double-talk. Seemingly meaningless, yet somehow everyone understands.

I make an effort to pull myself together. I glance at Kloucek, wondering if he's noticed that my mind has strayed from the Decision Support Tool to Donna's toenails. But Kloucek is clearly agitated about something in Donna's presentation.

"Yeah, yeah," Kloucek says, stabbing his stubby fingers into the air for punctuation. "We get it. But what I can't figure out," he says, now looking directly at me, "is why after we've paid you guys all this money, the software still doesn't perform as advertised."

Why is Kloucek dredging this up again? Because it was Kloucek's idea to scale back the scope of the project.

I gaze out the window. The sun has now set. An eerie glow of orange and purple bounces off the sides of the nearby office buildings. For a moment, I think of Holly and feel sad.

I get it. Kloucek's bluffing. He screwed up, overplayed his hand. Markowitz was more interested in seeing this thing through than Kloucek thought. He thought the idea was to be able to tell everyone they had a Decision Support Tool. He never thought Markowitz might actually want to use it. Kloucek would be the white knight. Take credit for controlling the costs. Easy to do if you scale back the project enough, say to the point it doesn't actually do what it was originally intended to do. He's trying to cover his ass by blaming us for not providing enough features. Surely, he must know if all this bubbled up to Markowitz, we could provide notes and emails that prove it was Kloucek who insisted on scaling the project back. He needs me more than I need him.

"Michael?" It's Kloucek's voice again. "What have you got to say for yourself?"

"Are you kidding? The software does everything you asked it to do." This slips out before I can properly filter my thoughts. But once I say it, I'm not sorry. In fact, I realize I can say just about anything I want to Kloucek at this point.

"What's that?"

"I'm sorry. Of course, we'll provide the additional features you requested. I'll email Jonathan, and he'll send you the adjusted estimate."

"What do you mean, adjusted?" Kloucek stammers.

I ignore this last comment. "I'll work out the details with Donna," I say. "It'll take a couple of weeks."

Kloucek must know I'm on to him now. He claims to have another meeting and storms out of the conference room, but not before turning and wagging his index finger at me. He wants to say something but can only stand there wagging his finger some more.

"What was that all about?" Donna asks when he's gone.

"He was bluffing."

"Of course, he's always bluffing because he's always shooting himself in the foot."

"Sorry."

"Don't be. I wish I could have said it. But it would have gotten me in trouble. He'd get even with me. Tell me to work a weekend when he knows I have plans. That kind of thing. He's quite the petty tyrant."

"Why do you work for him? I've worked with you long enough to know there are plenty of other petty tyrants that would love to have you on their staff."

She smiles. "The devil you know and all that. Plus, he's very ambitious. No scruples to speak of. He'd sell his mother if it would promote his career. Sooner or later, one of the political appointees around here will recognize his gifts and hire him. Then he'll be out of my hair," she sighs.

I picture her life in my mind. I've managed to paste together some of the pieces. I know she's got a Labrador retriever and likes country music, which is surprising since she's been a city girl all her life. She seldom drinks, but when she does, it's a particular white wine that I can never remember the name of, only that it is foreign but not French, maybe Australian. She's never mentioned a husband or boyfriend. She's lonely. Probably as lonely as me.

"Shall we review the new features of the Decision Support Tool?" she asks.

"Okay."

We settle in to review each of the features point by point. Although, it is really just a formality since we've been through it so many times by this point. With the exception of some very minor things having to do more with style than substance, we are in complete agreement.

"I'll email Jonathan with this," I tell her. "We should hear back fairly quickly. We estimated nearly all this for the current contract, before Kloucek scaled it back."

We shake our heads at the stupidity of Kloucek. We're gathering up papers when I'm startled to see that Cronin has somehow slipped into the room undetected. He's sitting in the row of chairs against the wall, chewing on a toothpick. He's dressed as he was before: black pants and a rumpled white shirt.

I nod to him. He gives me an indifferent look.

"Hey, sweetie," he says out loud to Donna.

"You can't talk to her like that," I start to say, but before I can finish, Donna's hand is on my arm, and her eyes are pleading with me not to say anything more.

Cronin abruptly stands up and starts toward the door. He says something out loud, not directed at Donna or me, almost as if he's talking to an imaginary person.

"Oh yes, I can. You better believe it," is all that I can make out. Cronin repeats this again, and then he's out the door.

"What a creepy guy," I tell Donna. But the color has left her face. "What's wrong?" I ask. "Look, I can talk to this Cronin and tell him to back off. I've dealt with his kind before."

"Please," she implores. "Don't do that. You don't know who you're dealing with. He's got a . . . a past."

With that, Donna gathers up her remaining things and hurries out of the conference room. I'm left angry and confused. Not at Donna, of course. At the fact that there are too many Cronins in the world.

COLD WAR 2

It's the wee hours of the morning. Crystal City is completely still. There's no breeze, no traffic, no miscreants slipping through the shadows. Just two lone tiny figures making their way up the pedestrian bridge from the airport. Each pulls a large suitcase with little, tiny wheels. Their flight from Tokyo was delayed in Los Angeles because the replacement flight crew was late arriving. They had no understanding of this. They just assumed it was due in some vague way to American inefficiency. They are an older couple with many wrinkles in their faces and worn looks in their eyes, worried that the hotel room they reserved has been given to some other tourists whose flight has landed on time.

They reach the hardened TV. Despite the hour, it is still on. There are scenes from the battle of Moscow raging in the background. The BBC narrator is saying, "The leaders of the Soviet Union, from Stalin and Khrushchev through Brezhnev, Andropov, and Chernenko, all rose from the ashes and rubble of the Second World War. Their worldview was molded in this crucible. Only Gorbachev, a mere lad at the time, did not share in this experience. The lessons learned by this generation explain much of the ruthlessness that characterized their reigns as first party secretaries."

The old couple stops at the hardened TV. They drop their luggage to rest for a moment. They've actually seen these scenes before, many times. It triggers memories from their own past—of a brother lost in the battle for the Philippines, of Hiroshima and Nagasaki, of the shame of a lost war. They are now very uneasy and wish they had stayed in Tokyo instead of coming to this strange land in which TVs constantly remind people of a past they would rather forget.

The voice coming from the hardened TV continues, "Take Brezhnev. During the Second World War, the Great Patriotic War as the Soviets call it, as the political commissar of the Eighteenth Army, Brezhnev reported to the commissar of the Ukrainian Front, Nikita Khrushchev. Khrushchev became Brezhnev's patron, took him all the way to the Politburo where he was in charge of the defense industry and the space program. Khrushchev made Brezhnev. Together they fended off the Stalinist old guard. Surely, Brezhnev was the one member of the Politburo that Khrushchev could count on to watch his back. But when Khrushchev was vulnerable late in his career, when even the Politburo had grown weary of his unpredictable behavior, when the Cuban Missile Crisis and economic stagnation had taken its toll, it was Brezhnev who was at the center of the conspiracy to bring down Khrushchev. A conspiracy that was eventually successful in 1964, overthrowing Khrushchev while he was off on holiday. Khrushchev spent the remaining seven years of his life under house arrest at his dacha outside of Moscow."

The old couple is now sitting on their luggage, staring transfixed at the hardened TV. The inner flame that had kept them on the move all day is now flickering. Each sits wondering how they will get up again, why they ever left their apartment, and whether their neighbor next door has remembered to feed their cat.

They watch numbly as Cold War images flicker across the screen of the hardened TV. Parades marching in front of the Kremlin, with missiles being towed, all painted with a red sickle and hammer. American fighter planes flying low over Russian frigates and destroyers headed for Cuba. President Kennedy speaking to the Senate about the Cuban Missile Crisis. Khrushchev gesticulating wildly on the floor of the U.N.

The old woman slides her hand into the old man's. He looks at her and gestures to the hardened TV. It's a gesture that says in Japanese: *It's the same old same old*. The old man slowly stands, pulling the old woman up. She smiles. They grab the luggage and start rolling it towards the other side of the pedestrian bridge. But first, the old woman stops and runs her fingers along the two interlocking circles spray painted on the hardened TV. *America is a very curious country*, she thinks.

HOLLY AT WORK

ROPES OF MIDMORNING LIGHT TWIST through the Library of Congress. Through the Asian Reading Room, down the Great Hall into the Catalog Center, deep within its bowels. Here, Holly sits at a large, metal, government-issued table. Her coat and backpack lay in a heap on the floor next to her. A laptop computer sits ready on the table. Mechanically, she thumbs through a large file of old letters and memorabilia.

Across the table, Ian, her co-worker, eyes her curiously. "What's wrong?" he finally asks.

"What?"

"You're flipping through those letters like there's no tomorrow."

"It's my father. He's such a bastard."

"Your father's alive?"

"Of course. But like I said, he's a bastard."

"Sorry. I just assumed he had passed away. You've never mentioned him."

Holly stops flipping through the file. She looks at Ian as if he's a child.

"That's because I hate him," she says slowly. "He ruined my life."

"How'd he do that?"

Holly pulls an object from the file. She identifies it, then makes an entry on her laptop.

"He's lied to me all my life. He killed my mother. Got drunk and crashed into a tree."

"That's horrible."

"It gets worse. I found out last night he may have been lying about that. I had dinner with my Uncle Jimmy. He said Michael may have staged it all. That it was my mother who was driving. That it was my mother who was drunk."

"Why would he do that?" Ian asks, but Holly's not listening. One of the letters in the file has captured her attention.

"My word," she says. Her jaw drops. "It's a letter of condolence to a Civil War widow. Signed by President Lincoln. It's just here in the middle of some routine War Department memos from World War One. Troop strengths, ammo stockpiles, that kind of thing."

A mischievous grin plays about Ian's lips. "Here's a thought," he says. "There's no one else around. It's just you and me. Just tuck that in your backpack. I won't tell. It's got to be worth a small fortune on eBay."

Holly eyes Ian. "Ill-gotten gains belong to the devil."

"What does that mean? Besides, you know I'm kidding, right?"

"Yeah right," Holly smiles. She appreciates the fact that Ian can find a way to amuse her even in the tomb-like environment of the card catalog room.

Moments pass. "Tell me again," Ian says, "why your dad lied to you about the car crash."

Holly flips the letter from Lincoln across the table in irritation. "He was trying to hide the fact they weren't getting along. I think they were on the verge of a divorce."

"But didn't your uncle say she had been drinking?"

"He probably drove her to it," she snaps.

But Ian presses on, "It doesn't make any sense. Why would your dad take the rap for the car wreck . . . in effect, taking the responsibility for killing your mom?"

"That's easy. To cover up the fact they weren't getting along."

"Look," Ian sighs, "I know guys like your dad. They're old school. Throw themselves on the grenade and all that."

They work in silence for a while until Ian's attention is diverted by the letter from Lincoln. His mind keeps coming back to it. Impulsively, he grabs the letter and shoves it in his pocket.

"What are you doing?" Holly asks in mock exasperation. Give me that. You'll crumple it. Then where will we be?"

"Come and get it," Ian laughs.

"Don't make me page the director."

"Oh, please, no. I know how cranky she gets when she has to get her big ass out of her swivel chair."

"You're incorrigible," Holly laughs despite herself.

Ian reaches into his pocket and pulls out the letter. With a deliberate motion, he tosses it back on the table. "Big bad director," he mumbles.

"Thank you," Holly says.

But Ian's mind has already returned to the mystery of Holly's father. "No, he says. It's like your uncle said. Your father was trying to preserve the memory of your mother. He was throwing himself on the grenade."

Holly bites her upper lip and says nothing. *Ian*, she thinks, *what does he know about growing up with a twisted past? With a father who killed your mother, or worse, lied about it for his own selfish purposes.*

She looks up at Ian. "Whose father does such a thing?" she pleads. "Real fathers don't tell lies. Yours would never do such a thing."

Ian laughs out loud. Too loud. It echoes off the stone columns in the card catalog room. "No," he says. "My dad only cleaned out the bank account and left my mom with three kids."

"Sorry," Holly says. "How old were you?"

"Five," Ian says. He reaches over, pushing some stray hair out of her face. He says, "Your dad just might be one of the good guys."

BEN'S DREAM

BEN'S BIG BODY TOSSES AND TURNS restlessly in the predawn chill of Crystal City. He sleeps beneath an assorted collection of rags. A paint-splattered drop cloth gathered from the never-ending renovation projects in Crystal City. A tattered peacoat from a sailor just discharged from the Navy. The sailor had stripped down to his briefs in the middle of Crystal Plaza and caught a cab somewhere. Ben was lurking in the shadows when it happened. The lunchtime crowd had a few laughs over it and then returned to their office cubicles. That's when Ben dashed out and grabbed the peacoat, but only the peacoat, not wanting to linger in full view on the plaza in broad daylight.

And then there's Shannon's scarf, which is always draped about his neck in one fashion or another.

Ben tosses about some more, throwing off some of the rags in his sleep. His eyes open bug wide, but just for a moment. "Not this time," he says out loud. He thrashes about some more, laughing maniacally. Then his eyes clamp shut. There's rapid movement behind his eyelids as he slips into a dream state.

It's an autumn afternoon, and football practice is winding up. Vivid fall colors fill the air. The sun is like a silver dollar, low in the sky. It's his senior year in high school. He's well on his way to setting the state's single-season record for receptions. There's a lot of talk about what they're going to do to their cross-town rival, Central. A lot of talk about what Ben's going to do to the Central defensive line.

They shower, get dressed, and make their way out of the locker room in small groups. There's more talk about Central, teammates patting Ben on the back, telling him he's the one that's going to show Central. Coach McTaggart is the last one out of the building, clipboard in hand. He comes over to Ben to discuss a play, then reminds Ben track and field practice starts in a couple of weeks and to dust off his discus. He's counting on him.

But now, in his dream, the sky darkens. Across the practice field, a large sedan pulls up to the curb. The driver's window slowly rolls down. A bony hand comes out and signals to Ben. It's Blue Ties. Ben wants to turn and run, to the locker room, to anywhere. But he knows that would be useless. There's no place to hide from Blue Ties and his minions.

Blue Ties rolls the window down further and pokes his head out. "How'd you like the party the other night? Heard you were a big hit with the ladies."

"Those were no ladies," Ben says. But he says this almost as a statement of fact and not accusingly. "They drugged me. Dr. Seagrove drugged me. Just like you do."

Blue Ties giggles, like a little girl. "Get in," he says. "It's time for your medicine."

"What if I don't?"

Blue Ties giggles again. "You know better than that."

"What if I just turn and run? You guys could never catch me."

"Oh my," Blue Ties says with mock indignation. "I hadn't thought of that. But then you would leave me with no alternative. I'd have to tell your mommy what a bad boy you've been. Did I mention we took some pictures at that party?"

"You sick bastard," Ben says. But he opens the rear door and slings his backpack in. One of Blue Ties' minions is sitting in the back seat. He's wearing a black suit and a black tie. Ben knows why he's there. He's in case Ben tries to get out of line, because Ben knows Blue Ties all by himself couldn't make him do anything.

Ben closes the rear door and the car eases from the curb.

"Yessiree," Blue Ties says. "We're making great progress. Just a few more injections, and we'll be done."

Ben snorts. "There's always more injections."

Blue Ties laughs, "Yeah. You're right." The man in the black suit remains completely silent, completely still.

One of the ladies from the party strolls by on the sidewalk. She peeks in the car and waves at Ben, even though her husband is right there with her. Ben gives her the finger. She reacts with mock indignation.

They speed down the long boulevard that runs through the middle of town. Ben decides the time has come to end it, to escape the clutches of Blue Ties. *So what if they got pictures*, he thinks. *I was drugged. Mom would understand. Besides, Mrs. Seagrove would never agree to let pictures like that get out.*

But then he wonders if Dr. Seagrove and Mrs. Seagrove are really married; maybe they're like the guy in the black suit, minions for Blue Ties. *It doesn't matter*, he thinks. *I only have one option. To run.*

"Boy, you're all stinky and sweaty," Blue Ties says over his shoulders as the car pulls up to a stoplight.

"Yeah. That's what happens at football practice. Like you would know."

Blue Ties' mood instantly changes. "I don't take shit from the likes of you. You got that?"

The man in the black suit beside him shoves an elbow into his side. "Got that?" Blue Ties says again.

"Got it," Ben mumbles, his anger like a hot coal burning in his chest.

"Louder," Blue Ties says as the car lurches forward from the stop light.

Ben knows he's in for another elbow in the side, but before the blow can be delivered and before the car can gain any more momentum, he throws the door open and hurls himself from the vehicle. He tries to break the fall by rolling, but pain stabs through his shoulder.

The car screeches to a stop, but Ben is already up and racing away. He runs down an alley, then turns down another alley. There's a high cinder block wall at the end, but that doesn't slow him down. With two bounding steps, he takes the wall and vaults over the top. He's amazed at how easy it is. He laughs out loud. The injections have done their job.

For a moment back in the alley, he shivers, wraps Shannon's scarf tighter, and struggles to wake, but the dream continues. He finds himself in someone's backyard. There's a chain link fence, then another, and then another. In the distance, he hears tires squealing. *Blue Ties*, he thinks. He takes the backyard fences with his best hurdling style. There is a sense of freedom in all this. It's almost fun, despite his desperate flight.

The squealing tires become more distant as he cuts down an overgrown gravel alley. He bends over, his lungs crying for air. "No more injections," he says out loud as he collapses with his back against a rundown storage shed.

Ben wakes. Early morning delivery trucks are now rumbling through Crystal City. Light starts filtering through the gritty city air. Ben sits bolt upright. He looks frantically around and realizes he's been dreaming again. He smiles, because the dream has a happy ending. No more Blue Ties. Then he frowns, because there really was no happy ending. He remembers how things really turned out. Instead of turning down the gravel alley, he headed back into town, to the courthouse, thinking the police would save him from Blue Ties. He tries not to think about it again but can't help himself. He bounds up the courthouse steps, five, six at a time, certain he's headed for freedom. Too late, he sees Blue Ties standing at the top, taking rapid drags from a cigarette. Ben can tell he's pissed.

"Always got to do things the hard way," Blue Ties shouts down at Ben. He flicks his cigarette, and the burning ashes scatter down the steps.

He spins to race down the steps, but there is the minion in the black suit. He looks to either side and there are the very cops he thought would help him. They all converge on Ben, but he doesn't go peacefully. The cops get slung off immediately, but the minion is bigger, tougher. But Ben can tell he's getting the best of him. He's about to toss him aside too when he feels a sharp pain in his thigh. Things start to move in slow motion, his head nods. *Fucking Blue Ties*, he thinks as his legs buckle beneath him. *Fucking injections*.

THE BAR AROUND THE CORNER

IN CRYSTAL CITY, there is a bar around every corner. Bars for young federal employees. Bars for old federal employees. The young drink because they're young. The old drink from the emptiness of supporting a rotting bureaucratic structure, designed to advance political careers without solving any real problems. Others drink for much darker and more sinister reasons. Out of bitterness. Out of hatred. Because the system gave them a taste of power, a taste of invincibility, and then took it away. Chopped them off at the knees just as the battle was about to turn their way. These habituate the seediest of the bars. They drink to nurse their bitterness, a bitterness that inevitably turns inward, into self-loathing.

Cronin sits at a bar far removed from the trendy ones of the young, or the slowly decaying bars of the old. It is literally on the other side of the tracks, in the no-man's land between Crystal City and the airport. The bar is so seedy it has no name. A sputtering neon sign above the door of the establishment simply says "Bar," the only clue that this is a place where even the likes of Cronin can get a drink and find some human contact. Albeit, some very seedy human contact.

Inside, there's very little illumination. Just some images flickering across the screen of a beat-up TV at the end of the bar and an incandescent light behind the bar. There are also foot lamps aimed at a stripper going through her gyrations on a stage in the corner. Cronin pays her no mind. His attention is completely focused on the shot glass in front of him.

He lifts the shot glass and salutes the bartender. "To the good old days," he says. "May they never come back to bite us in the ass." He throws the shot down the back of his throat. "What's in this again?" he asks.

"You don't want to know," the bartender answers.

"Oh yeah. Maybe I do. Maybe I'll just jump over this bar and beat it out of you."

The bartender turns one eye from the TV. "Look, pal. It's like I told you before. I get any more shit from you and no more booze."

"Just kidding," Cronin says, then turns quickly to watch the stripper. Not out of any need to see a scantily clad woman, just because it's the only thing going on in the bar.

In the background, the nightly news has just come on the flickering TV. Cronin is still lazily watching the stripper when something on the news catches his attention. He spins on his bar stool and rivets his attention on the TV. The announcer is saying, "Sad news in the world of sports today. Carson Runion has passed away at the age of sixty-five. One of the premier middle-distance runners of his generation, he is perhaps most remembered for a race he never ran, the fifteen hundred meters in the 1980 Moscow Olympics. Widely regarded as the favorite for the gold, he was bitterly disappointed when President Jimmy Carter announced the United States would boycott the Olympics over the Soviet presence in Afghanistan. Carson's loyalty to the United States was questioned by many when he criticized the boycott, saying: 'Why should the athletes be the ones to pay the price?'"

Cronin laughs out loud. It's an odd, choking laugh. He shouts at the TV, "Yeah, pal, we were all disappointed by that one. That fucking Carter screwed the whole damn thing up."

The bartender comes over. "You want another drink?" he asks.

"You bet," Cronin says, shoving his almost empty shot glass across the bar.

"Then quit talking to the TV. I've warned you about that before. You'll scare the trade away."

Cronin looks around. "What trade?" he snorts. Then adds, talking to no one in particular, "Yeah, that fucking Carter screwed the kitty good."

In the corner of the bar, the stripper sways her hips a few more times and literally grinds to a halt. The bumping and grinding music stops; the foot lamps dim. The stripper tosses her hair back, then slips into a worn satin robe.

She skips over to the bar and sits down on the stool next to Cronin. "You like my dancing?" she asks.

Cronin shrugs.

"You don't say much, do you?"

Cronin shrugs again.

"How about buying a working girl a drink?"

Cronin digs into his pocket and pulls out a big wad of bills. He hands the stripper a couple of twenties.

"You shouldn't carry that much money around in this neighborhood," she tells him. "Someone might take it from you."

"Last person who tried got his nuts stuffed in his mouth."

"How'd you get all that money?"

"The old-fashioned way. I killed people."

"You Mafia?"

"Worse than that. Federal employee."

"Well, anyway," the stripper says, "thanks for the money."

Cronin gets off the bar stool. Tosses some bills across the bar to pay for the drinks. "Thanks for staying the hell out of my hair," he says to the stripper. He heads for the door. Stops and grabs his overcoat off a wobbly coat rack. He drapes the coat over his arm. He's still for a moment. Shakes his head side to side and steps out into the night. A thin, crescent moon smiles down on him. "Fucking Carter ruined the whole beautiful plan," he says to the moon. "Fucking politicians."

HOLLY AT HOME

It's dark outside, and Holly is alone in her small townhouse. The wind from the river blows tree branches against her windows. She sits in her favorite chair, a large, overstuffed affair with extra thick arms. Shoes are off, legs folded up. Gas logs hissing in the fireplace.

Unpleasant thoughts intrude as she sips her wine. Like how she'd rather have real wood logs that pop and sizzle instead of the monotonous gas logs. How her life is not turning out like she planned. She's thirty. Should have at least one divorce under her belt. At least a van filled with kids on their way to soccer practice. Maybe she needs a man. Someone like Ian, but maybe more serious.

Her thoughts grow darker. *How could I ever have a relationship with anyone? With a father like Michael, I'm lucky I'm not locked up in an insane asylum. Uncle Jimmy says he was protecting me from the truth, but the lie is even worse. How could I ever trust any man? Little girls should not grow up without a mother. That's got to be someone's fault. If not Michael, who do I blame? God? Bad karma?* Indignation boils up within her.

But finally, the wine, the flickering gas logs, the tree branches scraping against the windows, do their job. Holly's eyes grow heavy; her head bobs as she tries to remain awake. But it's no use. She's dozing.

There's a kaleidoscope of dreams. She's a little girl riding a tricycle. A man running along behind urging her on. They're laughing. Now she's sitting in front of the TV. Happy until voices start to rise in the bedroom. A door slams, angry footsteps are heard in the hallway, a car roars off. She starts to cry quietly but refuses to wipe the tears from her eyes. Then there's an empty boat floating down a rapidly flowing river, empty oarlocks creaking. The rain comes down hard. The boat scraps against overhanging branches, gets turned sideways, takes on water, and starts to go under.

A gust of wind knocks over a neighbor's trash can. Holly stirs. She struggles to wake up, to investigate the noise outside, but she's too tired. Now, in her dreams, there's a grown woman. Holly suspects that she is the woman. She's in a wedding gown, inside a church. It's packed with people that she wants to believe are her friends, but she doesn't recognize any of them. Up front at the altar, there's a preacher and a groom. Both out of focus.

The church is old with paint peeling off the walls and bats circling about high up in the steeple. It's night outside, and the darkness penetrates through the old stained-glass windows. The woman stands at the back of the church, a bouquet of flowers in her hands. Even though people are talking to each other, there's no noise, like a silent movie. A man joins her and links his arm with hers. Michael? He nudges her, and they begin to march down the aisle. Everyone rises and looks at her. There should be processional music from an organ, but there is complete silence.

She takes a step. Pauses. Takes another step. Pauses. She glances from one side of the aisle to the other. People are happy for her. Smiling. Crying. Some are even clapping. All without sound. The preacher and the groom come into focus. The preacher has a shaved head and a crooked smile; the groom looks like Ian, but with a twisted, more sinister face.

Another step. Pause. They are almost to the front of the church. The man marching her down the aisle leans over, lifts her veil, and kisses her on the cheek. She can tell it's some type of parting gesture, silently saying: *I'll step aside while you get on with your life. Don't forget to call from time to time.*

Another step. Pause. A few more steps and she will be at the altar repeating vows. There's a blur of motion from one of the front pews. The man beside her becomes rigid, like stone. A woman stands in the aisle blocking her way. She's wearing a black velvet hat that obscures her face. She's waving a huge purse back and forth. She's gesticulating wildly. She's obviously drunk.

She can't hear what the woman is saying at first. Then suddenly all is sound and commotion.

"I won't allow you to do it!" the woman shouts. "He'll rob you of your youth. Your joy. Saddle you with kids. *Kids* for Christ's sake."

The man beside her reaches out with his free arm and shoves her back. Other men are now restraining the woman, pulling her back out of the way.

They start towards the altar again, but the woman breaks free. She's hissing in her ears, "Forget the career, forget world travel, forget a moment to yourself lingering over a martini, the stares of young men as you walk down the street."

The men bring her under control again. "I had a kid once," she's shouting with her arms pinned behind her. "Never a moment's rest. Always needing something."

Even though she can't see her face Holly realizes the woman is her mother. And in her dream, she breaks free from the man beside her, throws the flowers down, stumbles over her bridal train, and flees the church into a wild wind-tossed night.

Sitting in the big armchair, Holly's arms flail about wildly. She pulls herself out of the dream and wakes. Although she seldom remembers anything she dreams, she remembers this one.

She recalls the conversation with Uncle Jimmy. Her father did it all for her? All the lies, deceptions. What's worse: a mother who drank or a father who lied about it?

It's getting late, but she calls Michael's cell phone anyway. The phone stops ringing. There's silence at the other end.

"Michael?"

"Holly . . . Is that you?"

"Meet me at Bistro Bistro tomorrow night at eight. It's in the underground mall across from Crystal City."

"What time is it?"

"It's late."

"What's this all about?"

"Just be there."

"Has Uncle Jimmy been talking to you? You know you can't believe everything he says."

"Just be there."

Holly hangs up. I must be crazy, she tells herself. What can he possibly say that could ever make things right?

BISTRO BISTRO

LOOKING AT MYSELF in the mirror of the hotel bathroom, the artificial light leaves me feeling empty, like I'm not really there. My mind a stranger even to itself. With great effort, I take a towel and wipe a tuft of shaving cream from my ear. Grabbing the key card off the counter, I head out of the hotel room, out the lobby, and onto the street. I pick my way through the stalled rush hour traffic and early evening pedestrians to the underground mall that snakes its way beneath Crystal City. The entrance reeks of the stench of the homeless, their gray presence always lurking in the shadows. I pass shop after shop, selling everything from designer teas to bagels to narrow fuzzy ties representing one Scottish clan or another. Who the hell buys this crap? Even if I was Scottish, why would I want some cheap-ass tie that makes me look like a clown?

I continue on, deeper and deeper into the mall, until at last there are no more twists or turns. Still no restaurant. Yet there's the tinkling of silverware and the chatter of people. I realize there is some type of optical illusion with the walls, and there is yet one more turn. I proceed down a short, poorly lit hallway and find Bistro Bistro. Peering into the one window, I see Holly sitting alone at a table. She's sipping a glass of water, tapping her fingers on the table.

I want to leave. I suspect no matter what I say tonight the outcome will be the same. Holly will still hate me. I'm not encouraged by her expression. Since she was little, the faint little smile that is now stenciled on her lips always meant she was in no mood for nonsense. It's the same little smile she had on her face when she cross-examined me about Santa Claus, about why I had let her go on believing when half the second grade knew there was no such thing and that it was just parents putting on a big show for their kids. That she just felt like a stupid fool. I smile sadly at the memory.

I only enter Bistro Bistro when I realize this is probably my one, my only chance to make things right with Holly. I give a quick nod to the hostess as I pass and make my way through the restaurant to the table in the back.

"Hi," I say to Holly, acting as natural as I can, suppressing the fact that it's been at least a year since I've spoken with her face to face.

"Hi," Holly says without looking up.

"You look great," I tell her. "It's been too long."

A waiter comes over to take our order. "Anything to drink," he asks indifferently. He taps his pencil on the order pad.

Holly ignores the waiter. "Why didn't you tell me the truth," she asks. Loud enough that people from other tables look over. "Do you even know what the truth is anymore?"

"You've been talking to Uncle Jimmy, haven't you?" Of course, I know the answer to that. Only Uncle Jimmy and I know what really happened that night.

"Drinks?" the waiter asks again. It's obvious he wants to get on with it.

"How about two glasses of a nice Napa red," I tell him.

"Fine with me," he says and marches off in a huff.

"The truth is . . ." I start to say but have to stop. What is the truth? Why did Jimmy and I remanufacture the truth on that night so long ago? Did I think we could play God? Was it in some way to cover up the problems in our imperfect marriage? I finally say the only thing I can say, "I wanted to protect my little girl."

"From what? The truth about my own mother? Was she so evil?"

"Of course not," I tell her. "I loved your mother. She loved me, at least most of the time. But we had . . . problems."

"What kind of problems?"

"It was just that your mother always wanted more."

"More of what?"

"More of everything. She wanted to experience everything life had to offer. She wanted to go to all the parties. To travel everywhere."

"What's wrong with that?"

"Nothing, except we couldn't afford it on my salary; and there was the drinking. And I'm not talking about social drinking. Your mother never did anything in half measures. And when she was in a drinking mood, it could go on for days. I once got a call from a bartender in Richmond to come pick her up."

"And I guess you were just the perfect husband, the perfect dad."

"Of course not. I did things to your mom that I wasn't proud of. But by the time you came along, I had come to realize the quarter acre lot and the pigtailed little girl was enough for me."

"You beat my mom?"

"No. Of course not. But she needed help. And I knew it, but I did nothing. I didn't want to face the truth. That our lives were anything less than perfect."

"So you killed her with your indifference."

"No. No. At least, I pray that's not the case. Despite our problems, things were getting better. I felt like we had worked through the worst of it. But that night, the night of the Hackenworths' party, it all came bubbling back to the surface. Your mother was drinking. The Hackenworths were known to be good hosts, and there was always plenty of booze at their parties. She accused me of ruining her life, called me a control freak, told me she wished we'd never met. Even though I knew it was the vodka talking, I still got mad and told her to go to hell."

"Why did you let her drink so much?"

"Getting between your mother and a bottle of vodka could be hazardous to your health. Believe me, I know. She once threw a martini in my face just for telling her to slow down. Plus, like I said, things were getting better, and I didn't want to be the bad guy again."

Holly takes a deep, world-weary sigh. "So you told her to go to hell. That makes a lot of sense, Michael."

"No, no. It wasn't like that. She was getting that look in her eyes. I knew I couldn't stop her. Plus, I was mad at myself for not realizing sooner how much she'd been drinking. Uncle Jimmy tried to warn me, but I just didn't want to believe it. Like I said, things had been going so well for us."

"According to Uncle Jimmy, she ended up with her car wrapped around an oak tree."

I can sense the disapproval in her voice. "I would give anything to relive that night," I tell her. "Especially the part where I told her to go to hell. She tore out of the living room, where we had all gathered. I had an uneasy feeling things were about to get worse. It was Uncle Jimmy that remembered I had left the car keys in the pocket of my overcoat. But it was too late. We heard the car speeding off, spraying gravel all over the place. It must have been at that point that I realized it was raining, a heavy drizzle. 'We have to go after her,' Uncle Jimmy told me. 'How? In minutes, she could be on Ninety-Five headed to New York or Miami,' I told him. But he insisted we had to try. That I'd never be able to live with myself if we didn't. We got in Jimmy's car and headed out on the parkway. As we drove, the rain came down harder and harder. The car was whipped with sheets of rain. You've driven the parkway. You know how many sharp curves it has. We almost missed her; the windshield was just a blur. But after we had gone through the s-curve near Old Town, I realized there was a break in the row of boxwoods we had just passed. We circled back and pulled over. From there we just followed the car tracks. The car was literally wrapped around a huge oak tree. The front was completely crumpled. Steam was hissing from the radiator. The smell of gasoline was in the air. Your mother was still conscious. But I could tell she was fading fast. Her hair was matted with blood, I remember that. I remember the sickly-sweet smell from all of the blood. It trickled slowly from her ears. Somehow, I was able to force the driver's door open. I squeezed in beside her. Held her to me. Told her help was on its way. And in fact, it was because I could hear sirens in the distance. She looked up. Smiled weakly, as if to say I'm sorry, and rubbed my face with the back of her hand. Then she said one word."

"What was that?"

"Holly."

"What did she mean?"

"I don't really know. I've thought about it so often. There was so much in that one word. 'Take care of our daughter. Too bad I can't be there to see her grow up. I love you both.' At least that's the version I like."

Holly bangs her glass of water down on the table. She scoots her chair back like she's about to leave. "You're lying," she spits. "I saw the pictures in the old newspapers in the attic. You were driving."

I realize that the restaurant has become unusually quiet. There's no silverware clinking. No idle chatter. Without looking around, I sense that all eyes are on Holly and myself.

"Please. Don't leave. At least not yet. I'll never know if what I did was right or not. The sirens were closing in. If I couldn't make things right for her while she was living, maybe I could make it right for her in death. I got Uncle Jimmy to help me. 'Why are we doing this,' he asked me. 'I don't want my little girl to grow up thinking her mom was a drunk,' I told him. We moved your mom over to the passenger side. 'Hit me,' I told Jimmy. But he refused. We didn't have time for a debate, so I slapped him hard in the face. He slugged me in the mouth. 'Thanks,' I said. Then I crawled into the driver's side, told Jimmy to get lost and waited. The cops and reporters took care of the rest."

Holly is quiet. Everything is quiet in Bistro Bistro. No tinkling of silverware. No clatter of dishes. There's no dinnertime chatter. "Why did you take the blame?" Holly asks. Her words are measured, like a hunter drawing down on her prey.

I have the uneasy feeling that no matter how I answer, it's going to be the wrong answer.

"I thought a little girl should not grow up remembering her mother as a drunk. I thought maybe someday you might forgive me; I wasn't sure you could ever forgive your mom."

Holly grabs her purse and stands up abruptly. I can tell by her look, a look I'd seen many times when she was growing up, that I'm about to get an earful.

"Who knows what to believe from you," she hisses. "You're so used to twisting the truth you wouldn't know it if it spit in your face." Then she turns and rushes out of the restaurant.

I race after her, pausing only to hand the maître-de a wad of bills to cover our drinks. I pause outside the restaurant and look up and down the underground mall. There's no sign of Holly. I race back through the mall the way I came in, figuring Holly probably had to come in from the same direction. I try to sort through it all as I run. Was Holly mad at me for what happened to her mom, or mad because I lied about it all these years? Or was she just so used to hating me that she reacted in the only way she knew?

I turn into a blind corner and see Holly trapped by a huge man. It's Ben. She has a frozen look of horror on her face. I hear Ben asking her if she's seen Blue Ties.

"Please let me by," Holly says, but she is barely audible and clearly frightened.

"I just want to know if you've seen Blue Ties," Ben asks again.

I walk up. "Hello, Ben," I say softly.

"Hi, Michael," Ben says. "Have you seen Blue Ties?"

"No. But I've got a mint for you."

Ben takes the mint. "Thanks, Michael. You're alright." Then he ambles away.

"What was that?" Holly asks.

"He's homeless. I met him one night when I couldn't sleep. Too many dreams about your mom. About you."

"Who's this Blue Ties he was asking about?"

"I don't know for sure. I think he's just a figment of his imagination. Someone he can blame all his problems on. Claims he was the mastermind behind some grand conspiracy."

"He scares me," Holly says.

"He's harmless. At least I think he's harmless."

Holly's attitude seems to have softened. "Let's try again sometime," she says. "I have a lot of questions about my mom."

"Sure."

A VERY GRAY DAY

ALL IS GRAY IN CRYSTAL CITY. Gray clouds scud across the tops of buildings. Gray streets spin off into the distance, into the blank horizon. The gray mood fills the conference room. I sit and listen to Kloucek complaining about our new estimate for the optimization module.

Markowitz is also there. So is Donna.

And so is Cronin. He's sitting quietly in the far corner reading a folded-up newspaper, apparently unaware of the meeting now going on.

"These enhancements are way out of line," Kloucek says. "I'm disappointed, Michael. What are you people trying to pull?"

This, of course, is for Markowitz. So that Kloucek can show him he's a no-nonsense guy. I nod politely, shrug my shoulders, pretending to act at least a little bit guilty. But I know, if anything, the enhancements are underpriced. That Jonathan didn't want to rock the boat. "They're our best customers," he told me over the phone. "We want to keep them happy."

"What I can't understand," Markowitz complains, "is why these features, the optimization module especially, weren't in the first release."

I smile to myself. This ought to be good since Kloucek was the one that insisted they be taken out of the first release.

But Kloucek doesn't answer directly. Instead, he engages Markowitz in a sidebar conversation. All I hear are quick little whispers. But I know that somehow, we're getting the blame.

To hell with them. Bureaucratic fools. I turn to Donna and try to entertain her by making a goofy face. She looks back in mock disgust. I pick up the ink pen that is lying in front of me and pretend it's a rocket taking off. Donna stifles a laugh.

"Cut that shit out," Cronin blurts out from out of the blue and turns quickly back to his newspaper.

Kloucek and Markowitz both turn to Cronin, looks of concern on their faces. But quickly realize it's just Cronin. He's crazy and everyone knows it.

Except maybe not Markowitz since he's seldom in this corner of the building, seldom seen outside of his executive suite.

Kloucek is busy smoothing it over with Markowitz, telling him that Cronin is a retired civil servant who likes to hang out in his old office. That he's harmless. That it's best just to ignore him.

Their tone becomes more hushed. I can tell they are discussing the software again. Suddenly, they're quiet. Markowitz looks out the window, absorbed by the gray blankness outside, while Kloucek rifles furiously through a stack of folders laid out before him.

Kloucek's eyes dart to Donna. "Where's the timeline I asked for?" he says as if he's accusing her of something.

Donna gives him a blank look. "Everything you asked for is in the folders," she says.

I like the way she handles this. Atta girl. Don't let him bully you.

Kloucek brushes her last comment aside. "Well, it's not here," he tells her. "Run back to the office and get it. I need it now."

What an asshole.

Kloucek and Markowitz return to their huddled conversation. Donna rolls her eyes. I give her a look that says, *Oh well, what can you do?*

Donna makes her way through the empty chairs scattered about the conference room to the door. She's about to twist the knob when Cronin slams his paper down without warning and darts over.

He grabs Donna tightly by the wrist. "Not so fast, sister," he sneers. "This room is secure."

I'm out of my chair. Cronin's lost it completely. He's back in the Cold War back in some underground bunker plotting to overthrow communism.

Cronin's expression grows even more malevolent. He squeezes Donna's wrist tighter. "Please let go," she pleads. She's fighting back tears.

Cronin laughs. "You're a spy, he says. You know what we do with spies."

Kloucek sits twiddling his pen, as if he expects the situation to resolve itself. Markowitz just sits slack-jawed, astounded.

Now I have to do something. My first reaction is to take Cronin down, to tackle him, punch him in the nose, anything. But for some reason, maybe because Donna has hinted before that Cronin's shadowy past has included some serious martial arts training, I take another course of action. I ease over to the door.

"She's a spy," Cronin says again.

"I know, I'll take it from here," I tell him.

"How do I know you're not a spy?"

"After all the shit we've been through together? You know you can trust me."

Cronin is momentarily confused. He knows others are watching. "I guess you're okay," he says finally.

Slowly, I pry Cronin's fingers from Donna's wrist.

Cronin returns to his seat in the corner, picks up his newspaper, and starts humming a Sinatra tune from the fifties.

Donna turns and walks hastily towards her office, her high heels echoing through the empty hall.

"Don't forget the timeline," Kloucek shouts after her.

I retrieve my overcoat. "Meeting's over," I say quietly as I gather up my papers.

"Fucking contractors," I hear Kloucek say under his breath to Markowitz. "Can't trust them to be there when you need them."

Markowitz sighs out loud, probably wondering how the hell Kloucek ever got promoted.

Cronin is still sitting in the corner. "Christ. It's cold," he says. He shivers. "Must be Moscow. Only Moscow could be this fucking cold."

He looks directly at Kloucek. "Hey you," he says loud enough so that Kloucek has to turn and look at him. "Did I ever tell you about the time," Cronin pauses, looks up to the ceiling and laughs, "the time we tried to take Gorby out at the Olympics? With a discus thrower if you can believe that."

"I don't think I've heard that one," Kloucek says nervously, now ready to get out of the room as quickly as possible.

But me, I'm frozen. There's a familiar ring to Cronin's ramblings. I've heard this kind of talk before but can't remember where.

Cronin goes on now as if no one is there, "Fucking Carter ruined the whole glorious plan, ruined all the fun with his goddamn boycott. Boy, did that put a monkey wrench in the deal." Then he sits motionless, like stone, frozen in a moment from the distant past.

I start out the door. Kloucek and Markowitz are gathering their papers, in a rush to get out before Cronin comes out of his trance.

On my way out of the building, I stop by Donna's desk. She's putting on an overcoat and bundling up.

"You okay?"

"I've told Kloucek before," she says, "Cronin makes me nervous."

"Why doesn't he call security or something?"

"Because he's afraid of him. Everyone's afraid of him. I don't think he even has a job with our agency. There are all sorts of rumors going around like he used to work for some black-funded secret agency."

"Why does he keep hanging out in that one conference room?"

"They say his office used to be in there, before they took down the walls and expanded it into a conference room."

BEN AT COLLEGE

A DRY WIND SWIRLS through the old oaks scattered about the campus, kicking up tiny whirlwinds of dust and debris.

Inside the student union, a couple sits on a tattered couch, paying little attention to the TV images that flicker before them. She slings a purple scarf about his neck. "Come on," she says. "Tell me. I'm dying to know. How'd you do?"

"I got gold," he tells her.

"Ben, that's great," she says, trying to pull him to her with her scarf. But he resists. He doesn't feel like playing along.

"You're no fun," she says. "Ben, smile. You got the gold. It was a really big meet, too. Right?"

"Pan Am Games," Ben says flatly. "It doesn't get much bigger. Only the Olympics."

"Come on. Be happy."

"I just don't feel like it, Shannon."

"I don't understand you. You should be happy."

"I almost got DQ'd."

"What?"

"Disqualified. They made me pee into a cup—with someone watching."

"A urine sample."

"Yeah. They said I flunked."

"It was a mistake, right?"

"I don't know. Blue Ties took care of it."

"Your coach? He took care of it? Ben, that doesn't make any sense."

"Coach Callahan's my coach. Blue Ties, he's my adviser. He fixes things."

"So he explained to them that there was no way you were taking any drugs or anything?"

"I don't know. He just fixed it."

"But you're not taking any drugs?"

"Who knows? They make me take so many things."

"But Ben, you can't take drugs. That'll get you in trouble. You'll get banned."

"Blue Ties takes care of all of that."

Then Ben is silent. Like he's said too much. Shannon retrieves her scarf and folds it up. She lays it in her lap, scanning Ben's face for any sign that maybe she has misinterpreted what he's said.

"Must be nice to have someone fix things for you," she finally says.

Ben looks at Shannon like she's from another planet. "No, it's not. It's anything but nice," he tells her. "He makes me do things I don't want to do."

"You mean he trains you too hard?"

"No. Worse than that. Much worse."

Shannon takes his hand and holds it to her lips. "What then? Please tell me."

"I can't. It's a secret plan."

"But you can tell me. I'm your girl, aren't I?"

"Sure you are. You're the best thing that's ever happened to me."

"Then," Shannon implores him, "please tell me what it is this Blue Ties jerk wants you to do."

Ben hangs his head. "I can't. He'd kill me. There's a pause. Worse than that, he'd kill you."

Shannon hits him playfully in the shoulder. "Stop kidding," she says. "You're scaring me."

But Ben knows he's not kidding. Blue Ties in fact would kill them both if he ever told the plan. He's about to explain this to Shannon when the flickering TV images catch his attention. President Jimmy Carter is on the TV. It's a press conference. He's saying because of the Soviet aggression in Afghanistan, the United States, regretfully, has no choice but to boycott the 1980 Olympics in Moscow.

Ben buries his head in his face. "No. No. No," he says. "Blue Ties is not going to like this. Not one bit."

Shannon lifts Ben's head and looks into his eyes. "Ben," she says, "please tell me what's wrong. It can't be that bad."

Ben looks wildly around. He points at Jimmy Carter's image on the TV. The press conference is wrapping up, and Jimmy Carter is taking questions from the press: "Won't the Russians retaliate by boycotting L.A. in '84? What about the athletes? All the training down the drain? Are our allies with us?"

"Blue Ties will blame me for this," Ben says. "I know he will."

"The Olympic boycott? How in the world can he blame you for that? Besides, it's just another track meet. It's not life or death."

Ben snorts. "You don't understand. We had something planned for Mr. Gorbachev."

"The prime minister?"

"Mr. Brezhnev is the prime minister."

"Then who's this Gorbachev?"

Ben takes a deep breath. Then carefully chooses his words, like he's reciting something from memory. "Blue Ties says he's an up-and-comer that doesn't want to play ball." He glances out the plate glass window. A black limousine is pulling up to the curb. A man in a gray suit, well-groomed with a receding hairline, emerges. He's wearing a baby-blue tie that contrasts oddly with the gray suit. The man adjusts his sunglasses and walks briskly toward the student union building.

"You've got to get out of here. Now."

"I'm not going to leave you like this."

Ben grabs her shoulder. Shakes her to the point that she tells him he's hurting her. "Leave now," he tells her. "Before it's too late."

Shannon tugs the lavender scarf that is still hanging about Ben's neck. She loops it around one more time, like a mother preparing her child to play in the snow. She leans over and kisses his cheek. "Call me when the real Ben can come out and play," she whispers in his ear. Then she's gone.

Down a distant hall of the student union building, Ben hears a door clang open. He hears the sound of black Oxford shoes slapping smartly down the hallway. He grabs his knees and starts rocking, faster and faster.

RIVER WALK

WITH AS MUCH ENERGY as I can muster, I stride past the hardened TV on the pedestrian bridge over the highway. I'm in athletic shorts and running shoes. It's late afternoon. The scheduled meeting with Donna and Kloucek was postponed at the last minute because Kloucek went off to an awards ceremony with Markowitz and the assistant secretary. Some mutual admiration thing where everyone pats themselves on the back while the country slips another notch down the spiral of decay and corruption. To hell with all that. It's a great day to be alive.

I walk on the jogging trail that runs along the river. Federal workers out for their daily workouts are everywhere. Grim looks of determination on their faces. Looks that say we're in complete control of our lives. We know where we're going; nothing can stop us. It's the look Helen used to have in the early days, before the booze and the craziness caught up with her. If they only knew what pawns we really are. How little control we have over our own lives.

Sunlight reflects off the ripples in the river. The trail loops near a marina, with rows and rows of boats gently bobbing with the waves. There's a large daysailer with two couples drinking wine and joking back and forth. One of the women is particularly attractive, with dark hair and an air of grace. She's laughing gaily at something one of the men said. No doubt something suggestive. If she knew the future, would she be so happy? If she knew he would be broke in five years, would that change things? Maybe it's best just to go from moment to moment. High expectations can be bad for your health.

Everything is conditional. With knowledge comes change. If I had known how things would end with Helen, would I have married her? Maybe if I knew I'd have all those years with Holly, watching her grow.

I jog for a while. Young women in running shorts and athletic tops zip by like I'm just another inconvenient obstacle, like a misplaced stump in the road. I try to keep up with them, but quickly realize I'm way out of shape. I curse myself for letting things reach this point.

The sight of the young women jogging, the echo of laughter from the dark-haired woman on the daysailer, trigger long-repressed feelings. Since Helen, there's been no one else. With some sadness, I realize it's me; I'm damaged goods. I've never been able to move on after Helen. Burying myself in my work, raising Holly. There were women that were interested. Some damaged goods like me, trying to recover from broken dreams of happy families, of picture book holidays, of someday having grandkids. But unlike me, ready to move on, ready to rebuild their lives. Women like Donna, I realize.

For no reason, I say out loud, "Wouldn't change a thing. No sir."

I would still take the blame. A little girl should not grow up thinking her mom's a drunk. I knew the risks when I went down that road. Knew that someday she might find out the truth. Someday there could be hell to pay.

The trail takes me through some woods littered with some kind of public art project. What looks like parachute canopies are scattered throughout. Each canopy is a different color, all bright and reflective. Some very high up in the trees. Some suspended in the middle of clearings hanging by invisible cables. All very clever. The whole effect is there is some kind of invasion underway. In fact, there's a nearby sign that says, "Peace Invasion" and gives details of the artists and the thousands of dollars it cost.

The sun is low enough that blades of light slice through the canopy of trees. I squint to make sure I don't stumble on the cracked asphalt. I push thoughts of Helen and what might have been from my head. I breathe the cool air of the woods. But I can't get the image of parachutes out of my head. Wouldn't it be great if occasionally we could pull the ripcord and parachute out of our mistakes? Should I have pulled the ripcord on the lie Jimmy and I created for Holly?

The path emerges from the woods and bends back towards the river. The river broadens. The water flows with hardly a ripple. I walk over to a mossy bank and sit. I squint into the sun; the brightness is painful. I lie back and close my eyes. What if Helen hadn't driven off drunk that night? Could we have made it work? Probably not. Our life was too pedestrian for her. She was meant to travel to the stars, not change diapers, not play the part of the dutiful wife and mother. Say she lives, and we split up; do I get Holly? That was the best part of my life, watching Holly grow up. Being there to answer the endless questions about why boys were so mean, and why carrots were called carrots, and why did kids have to go to school anyway. Then the occasional question about her mom. "Tell me again, Daddy, what happened to Mommy?"

"The angels came and took her."

That worked for a while, a long while. It wasn't until middle school that she found the newspaper clipping in the attic and connected her mom's death with me. "It was a stormy night. I lost control on a wet road, and we crashed. Could have happened to anyone," I told her. But the jig was up.

"You killed Mommy. Why didn't you tell me?"

"I was going to tell you when you were old enough," I told her.

That was the plan all along, wasn't it? To keep Holly from finding out the horrible truth about her mom. Substitute another truth. It was an accident. It could have happened to anyone. But it was never the same after that. Holly walled herself off. I was no longer welcome.

A BOX OF LETTERS

DEEP WITHIN THE RECESSES of the Library of Congress Holly and Ian are at work in the Special Collections room. It's early, and the library is still closed to the public. Outside, the last of the rush hour traffic is busy sorting itself out. Inside, there are only muffled coughs, occasional chair legs scraping across the tile floor. There's a small sparrow trapped in the main reading room, unremarked upon by any of the library workers. It flits from one high nook to another, like a small, dark phantom.

Ian is systematically sorting through a recently discovered box, documents from the Carter administration. "The maintenance man found these behind the old coal-fired furnace in the basement," he tells Holly.

"I keep telling them we need to keep better track of this stuff," she retorts.

Holly is labeling books bequeathed to the library by a recently deceased senator. She finishes pasting a card catalog label on a book and slides it across the table. "Who's this guy kidding," she snaps. "A copy of *Das Kapital*? And over there is a copy of *Herodotus*. He never read any of this stuff. He was too busy drinking and chasing women."

Ian looks up from his task and laughs. "Fascists don't need to read," he says. "It only confuses them." Then he looks at Holly's face and adds, "Why the frowny face?"

"Sorry. Had dinner with Michael last night."

"Your dad?"

She tilts her head and gives Ian a look.

"Most people call their dad, their dad," he says.

"I prefer Michael. There's more emotional distance.

"How did it go?

"I walked out."

"Why? I thought you wanted to find out what really happened to your mom? And I thought your uncle Jimmie explained all that to you?"

"I wanted to hear it straight from Michael. But when he got into the details, what they had to do to pull it off, I ran. They lied to the police! And I still can't understand why he lied to me for so long about my mom."

"In some twisted way, I think he was trying to protect you."

"From what?" Holly exclaims, exasperated, throwing her arms up in the air.

"From the gossip. The rumors. Everyone's whispers about poor Holly. 'Did you hear about her drunk mom? Crashed into a tree. Killed herself.'"

"At least that's the truth. I could handle that better than being lied to all these years by my own father. I couldn't get past that. I walked out. I had to flee."

"Maybe, but you'll never know."

"Oh, I know alright."

"Really? Your dad made a split-second decision twenty years ago. He didn't want you growing up with the whole world knowing your mom was a drunk and killed herself stupidly in a car accident."

"That's playing God. What kind of arrogance is that?"

Ian puts aside his work. "Holly," he says with an intense expression on his face, "he was just trying to protect you. My dad caught the Greyhound out of town when I was five. I haven't seen him since. There's a lot worse than your dad."

They both resume their work. "So you're taking his side?" Holly says at last.

"Just saying there's a lot worse."

They continue working in silence. Holly's face reflects an inward struggle. "You know," she says at last, "I worry about him sometimes."

"Who?"

"Michael."

"I thought you hated him."

"I do. As a father. As a human being, I feel sorry for him. He's getting old, and he's by himself an awful lot. If he just had a lady friend. Someone to check up on him. Keep him fed. Keep him out of trouble."

"He's a big boy. He can take care of himself."

But Holly barely hears him. "Because he's so alone, he's developed some strange friends. Like last night as I was leaving after telling Michael off, this huge man, dressed in rags and obviously homeless, comes from out of nowhere and asks me for a light. I mean this man was big, six-five, maybe bigger. He had me cornered. I was scared. Then Michael comes along. For once, I'm glad to see him. But the man says, 'Hi, Michael.' Michael gives him a light, hands him a mint from the restaurant, and tells the man it's getting late and he ought to run along. But first the man goes into a rant about some CIA plot to assassinate Gorbachev."

"Gorbachev?"

"Right. At the nineteen-eighty Olympics. Claimed some guy named Blue Ties was in charge of the whole thing. It was Blue Ties this and Blue Ties that. I mean this guy was scary strange."

"That's impossible."

"I know."

"No. I mean it is literally impossible. That was the Olympics that Carter boycotted. Remember? Afghanistan and the Soviets?"

"Maybe. I'm not really into sports."

They're working in silence when their supervisor, Kendra, comes and asks Holly to help her with a display in the main reading room.

Holly turns and makes a funny face at Ian, who feigns an expression of hurt feelings.

Alone in Special Collections, Ian returns to the cardboard box of Carter memorabilia. He sorts the documents into government, personal, and miscellaneous piles. He picks up a memo to his staff encouraging them to be energy efficient, to set an example for the people of America. Another document is a press release of a visit to a nuclear sub berthed in New Haven, Connecticut, reminding people that Carter served on board a nuclear sub as a young ensign.

"Poor bastard," Ian clucks to himself. "These were the good times. Little did he know the energy crisis, the Iranian embassy, losing the '88 election, were all right around the corner."

Ian's about to shove the cardboard box aside and go down to the coffee kiosk in the basement for some green tea when he notices an envelope in the corner of the box.

"Son of a bitch," he whistles, plucking the envelope from the box and laying it before him like a prized jewel. It's got the librarian's seal on it, but it says Office of Research. *How curious*, he thinks. Addressed to Barbara Cohen who worked here they say oh so many years ago. "Why is this in the Jimmy Carter box, I wonder." He laughs and flicks the corner of the envelope and sends it spinning. "I have a feeling this is going to be good. I wish Holly was here."

The envelope stops spinning. He slowly pulls out a formal letter. It also has the librarian's seal and is addressed to a long-retired director of research. The letter is a response to a personal request from Jimmy Carter for information. Information on extraterrestrials, but not from the Office of Research, from the Vatican Library. Actually, requesting the director of research to use her personal connection with a friend with access to the Vatican's collection of extraterrestrial material to intercede on behalf of the president.

Ian is beside himself with glee. "Jimmy Carter, you crazy guy." He reads the last paragraph. The request is denied, and the letter goes on to say that the Vatican denied that any such collection on extraterrestrials existed in its library.

"Oh, Holly's going to love this," he says, carefully folding the letter and returning it to its envelope.

The small sparrow trapped in the main reading room has found its way to Special Collections. Much subdued, as if it has given up and is now ready to accept its fate. It finds a high ledge and perches, looking indifferently down on Ian.

THE PLAN

BLUE TIES SITS ON THE EDGE of a battered desk. Initials, threats of murder, and random designs have been carved into every inch of the desk. He blows a thin line of cigarette smoke in Ben's direction.

"You don't like it when I smoke, do you?" Blue Ties laughs.

Ben stares straight ahead, neither right nor left, at a blank spot on the far wall, sitting scrunched in a raggedy old armchair with puffs of padding erupting from odd places.

"Look at the big athlete now," Blue Ties goes on. "Champion of the Pan Am Games. Of course, wouldn't be champion without his ole buddy to set things right with the officials." He laughs and coughs at the same time. It's a deep, raspy, corrupt sound.

"I can win without your injections."

"Don't kid yourself. Without your medicine, you're just another also-ran."

"I'm not afraid of you," Ben says.

"What's to be afraid of? We're all friends here."

"We're not friends. You're my enemy."

"After all we've been through," Blue Ties chuckles. "After all of the planning. You hurt my feelings."

Ben clenches his fist at his side, the anger rising in his face, but he says nothing.

"Alright, Einstein. Let's go through it again. Step by step. One."

"One," Ben parrots, "I break the Olympic record and give the commies a lesson."

Blue Ties eyes Ben. "Fat chance," he says. "You DQ and head for the locker room."

"What does it matter?" Ben argues. "I know I can win. I'm number one in the world. Why can't I win then go to the locker room?"

Blue Ties gives a deep, dark laugh. "You never learn, do you?" He hops off the table and grabs two wires connected to a large marine battery and jabs the leads into Ben's shoulder blade. Despite himself, Ben winces in pain.

"Let's try again," Blue Ties says. "What's step one?"

"One. I DQ and return to the locker room."

"Good lad. You DQ because we don't want a lot of attention. You DQ, and you're instantly forgotten. It's the winners that the TV cameras follow. Two?"

"Two. Change into the security guard uniform."

"Right. Three?".

"Make my way to the VIP box where all the Central Committee members will be sitting."

"And?"

"Look for that Gorbachev guy."

Blue Ties hops off the table and slaps Ben hard in the back of the head. "His name doesn't matter, God damn it," he says. "Look for the guy with the weird birthmark on his forehead. The mark of the beast."

Blue Ties remains standing over Ben. "Four. You whack him. And what do you shout?"

"Ukraine forever."

"In Ukrainian!"

"Ukrayina navazdy."

"Close enough. Then what do you do?"

"Make my way to the river."

"Right. In the confusion, you use your prodigious, drug-induced strength and speed, scale down the stadium walls, and make your way to the river."

"Why do you want this guy out of the way? He wants to reform the system. Shouldn't we be supporting this guy?"

Blue Ties rolls his eyes. "You been going to class again? Watching public TV in the student union?" Blue Ties grabs the battery leads and shocks Ben in the shoulders again. "You know we hate public TV."

Ben's body twitches in contortion. "Fuck you," he spits out.

Blue Ties ignores all this. "You're exactly right. He is a reformer, and we don't like reformers. We like the status quo. More job security. Five?"

"What?" Ben says, still dazed from the shock.

"Five. God damn it." Blue Ties shocks him again. "Catch the commie log back to freedom. Say it."

"Catch the commie log back to freedom," Ben repeats, now breathing quite heavily, spittle coming from his mouth.

"Six?"

Ben doesn't wait to be shocked again. "Wait for the good guys under the bridge. They'll be there? Right?"

"If you do the job. But you'd better do the job. Or you won't have any place to run. You hear me, Mr. God Damn Pan Am Champ?"

LUNCH WITH DONNA

DONNA AND I WORK ALL MORNING on the final requirements for the optimization module. At lunch, we decide to eat at a place across the street in the underground mall. A place named Luna that plays a lot of psychedelic music from the seventies yet has plenty of meat and potatoes on the menu. We find a quiet booth in the back.

"Can you guys really make this thing work?" Donna asks.

"And then some," I laugh. "We've got a math PhD that develops all types of algorithms for us. Pay him peanuts, really. He was our UPS guy for years."

"No kidding."

"Really. He couldn't find a job in academia. Only thing he could find was driving for UPS. It was our secretary who suggested he apply."

"A rags to riches story?"

"Hardly. You know what Jonathan pays us."

"Right. It makes me glad I'm a government employee."

The waiter comes, and Donna orders an Asian salad with rice noodles and mandarin oranges. I order a grilled cheese sandwich with fries.

"How long have we been working together?" Donna asks.

"On and off, close to three years."

"Yet we know so little about each other. For instance, I never figured you for a grilled cheese."

"I'm a man of simple tastes. I try to limit myself to once a week, cholesterol and all that, and today's the day."

Donna becomes pensive. "You said you're estranged from your daughter?"

I fiddle with my silverware. "Wife died. Many years ago. Daughter won't speak to me."

"Sorry. Wrong question."

"It's okay."

"You don't have anything to do with your daughter?"

"She hates me because I lied to her about her mother's death. I was just trying to protect her."

"Still, you probably shouldn't have done that. Truth is usually the better road. No matter how painful."

"Yeah. I found that out the hard way."

"What was the lie?"

"It's so convoluted it'd take me all afternoon to explain. But my intentions were good. I wanted to protect my daughter from knowing what really happened to her mom."

"Okay."

"No, really. I'd like to talk about it. It's like I've been carrying around this huge stone on my back for years. She got drunk and drove and died in a crash. I tried to cover it up. But how about you? Any kids? A husband lurking somewhere?"

"One kid. One dead husband. Lung cancer. Smoked like a chimney. About ten years ago."

"Sorry."

"It was sad, but the truth is we were just staying together for the kid."

"What about the kid?"

"Anita. The light of my life. She's a marine biologist. Travels all over the world. Articles printed in journals. I don't know where she gets that from."

"Don't be modest," I tell her. "Anyone that can manage Kloucek the way you do must be a genius."

She laughs.

"No, really. I know his type all too well. You do all the work. He takes all the credit. If something goes wrong, you're the convenient scapegoat."

Donna plays with her silverware. "He has his good points," she says.

"Like what?"

"He's too busy brown-nosing Markowitz to micromanage."

We both laugh. The salad and the grilled cheese come. The conversation has sputtered, and we eat in silence. I don't know what to do with my hands, where exactly to look. I look out through the plate glass at the front of Luna. There is a face staring back. There's someone pointing at us, talking at us through the plate glass. With horror, I realize it's Cronin, and he's making his way into the restaurant. The hostess tells him he'll have to wait for a table. "Screw you," he says. He weaves his way back to our table.

"How's my pretty little spy?" he says to Donna, ignoring me.

I can tell that Donna is clearly uncomfortable. Cronin pulls up a chair and slides his arm around her shoulders.

I reach over to remove the arm, but Cronin, with catlike quickness, grabs my wrist. I try to pull my arm away, but Cronin tightens his grip. "That's it," I say. I get up, ready to strike Cronin with my free hand. Cronin emits a low growl, like a cornered animal.

Donna puts her hand out, a signal to me to stop. "Please," she pleads with Cronin, "leave us alone."

Cronin releases my wrist, tossing it aside. I sit back down. For a moment, we all sit frozen in our chairs, no one knowing what to do next. I'm looking at Donna. Donna's looking at her plate. Cronin's looking off somewhere into the infinite horizon behind my head.

With a shiver, Cronin gets up without a word and makes his way towards the front of Luna. The hostess tells him to have a nice day. "Fuck off," he says over his shoulder on the way out.

I lean over to Donna. "Why don't you let me deal with him? I can handle myself. I took karate in my younger days."

Unexpectedly, she takes my hand. "Oh, Michael," she says, "you don't know how dangerous he really is. He's been involved in political assassinations."

WHAT BEN SAW

BEN MAKES HIS WAY OUT of the shadows of the underground mall to claim a recently discarded half-eaten bagel lying just beyond the entrance of Luna. As he snatches up the bagel, he glances through the plate-glass window. He pictures himself with Shannon, sitting at a table, joking with the waiter about the day's special.

He spots Michael and Donna, then Cronin, all still frozen in time, at their table in the back. His mind screeches to a halt. He drops the bagel; his fingers scratch in his pocket for an old cigarette butt he's been saving. He lights it and inhales nervously.

"It can't be," he says out loud. "After all this time. The tables are turned, Blue Ties. Who would recognize this old ball of rags now?"

He squats low before the plate glass window. "Imagine that," he whistles. "You've been right under my nose all along." Then he notices Michael. "I thought you were my friend," he says. "But now I see you are in league with Blue Ties. You, too, must be dealt with. And that lady with you. All will be dealt with. Do you hear that, Shannon? At last, it's my turn. But all in good time. All in good time."

Then Ben hunches down, mixes with the lunchtime crowd, and disappears into the shadows of the underground mall.

Much later, past midnight, Ben settles into his tattered refrigerator carton under the pedestrian bridge. He's been foraging all day, but he's still restless. He wads up some old clothing under his head. He compulsively sniffs the purple scarf that Shannon gave him so many years ago.

He talks to himself. "Ben, you remember the plan. Yes. Well, tell it to me again." He's using two voices, one for himself and one for Blue Ties.

He conjures up a huge stadium in his mind. There are cheers from the crowd echoing through the stadium. There's a running event in progress. Pole vaulters are warming up. "Step one," he says in Blue Ties voice, "DQ and return to the locker room. Step two, change into the security guard uniform."

"DQ," he snorts in his own voice. "No more DQs."

Blue Ties voice, "One, you DQ and return to the locker room."

Ben's voice, "One, I DQ and return to the locker room."

Blue Ties voice, "Two, change into the security guard uniform."

Ben's voice, "Two, change into the security guard uniform."

Ben's voice again, "Bullshit. I've never DQ'd in my life. One, it's the finals. I've fouled twice. It's my last throw. The whole stadium is watching me, watching Ben. I take my time with the windup. Think about how much I hate Blue Ties. About how this throw will ruin his life. I pivot on my left foot. Drive to the center. Pivot on my right. Then explode into the throw. Control the reverse. Control the reverse. Don't foul. I swear the discus is headed out of the stadium. When it lands, before it has even skidded to a stop, the crowd erupts. They're cheering this brass young American. It's a new Olympic record. It's a gold medal. Two. My teammates lift me up on their shoulders. The crowd's still cheering. Brezhnev and Gorbachev come down from the VIP box. They embrace this brash young American. An era of peace is ushered in. Of course, I pass the drug test since I've only pretended to take Blue Ties' pills."

Then it's Blue Ties voice again, "You fucked up big time kid. Now we have no choice but to have you eliminated."

Ben's voice, "No. You fucked up, Blue Ties. You fucked up big time. Because I haven't been taking your mind control pills. What? You look nervous. You forget your muscle guys? You thought all you needed was your mind control pills, didn't you? Oh, don't tremble. I'll be quick about it; I'll be merciful. I'll be floating down the river, headed for home, before anybody ever figures out what happened to poor ole Blue Ties."

Then Ben laughs out loud, shaking his huge body in the refrigerator carton. Off in the distance, there's the rumble of a freight train. From somewhere he hears the laughter of some late-night revelers.

He rolls to his side. He squeezes Shannon's purple scarf under his head. His fingers linger on the thin threads. He closes his eyes and prays that sleep will come to him this night. "Michael. I thought you were my friend," he says softly into the scarf.

FLOATING THE POTOMAC

MY SHOES ARE OFF, and my pants are rolled up. I'm standing in the Potomac throwing paddles and life preservers into a rental canoe as it bobs on the ripples rolling in from the river. The feeling of sand and muck gushing between my toes is oddly exhilarating. I have the feeling I have broken out of my everyday rut, if only in this small way.

It's Holly's idea. A paddle downstream for several miles where her friend Ian has agreed to pick us up. I'm not sure what's supposed to happen in those few miles. Talk of serious things. Her mom. Why I lied about her all these years. All in all a very pleasant afternoon.

A small rusty pickup truck pulls into the parking lot. A young man I've never seen before is driving. Must be Holly and her friend Ian. Holly hops out as soon as the pickup comes to a grinding halt on the gravel.

"Looks like a good day for it," I tell her as she approaches. "Is that Ian?"

Holly shrugs. "Let's get going," she says. "Ian's going to pick us up at the Gunston Cove boat ramp."

I ask her if Ian is her boyfriend, but she doesn't respond. She busies herself arranging the gear in the canoe.

We put in. Holly is in front; I'm in back. "Let's see if I can remember that old J-stroke," I joke.

But Holly remains silent as we paddle out to midstream. In fact, all is silent. There's a mega metropolis bustling all around. But out on the river, there is only the sound of the water lapping at the canoe as our paddles propel us on and the whisper of a breeze in our ears. For a moment, I swear I hear Helen's voice drifting over the river. It seems soft and forgiving, but it's just the breeze and the rippling water playing tricks on me.

We reach midstream and rest the paddles across the gunwales. Holly suddenly turns to me. "Tell me something nice about my mom," she says.

"I'm not sure what you mean," I answer.

"I've got memories, but I think they're mostly things a little girl made up to make it through the night. I want a real memory. Something I know is true. There must have been a moment in time when we were a family, a normal family."

"Of course. Your mother, at heart, was a good person. But she fought many demons. I really believe if we could have somehow gotten through that night at the Hackenworths' party, we would have made it."

"Just give me my memory," Holly says. "I don't want to hear about the night my mom died again."

I look into Holly's eyes. My little girl is gone. Looking back is a grown woman trying to piece together the fragments of her life.

"There was one afternoon," I tell her, "that has always stuck in my mind. It was a perfect day, and your mom decided we should have a picnic in the neighborhood park. She actually said, 'It's time this little family of ours had a picnic.' She did all the preparation. We packed up some sandwiches, and we were off to the park."

"What kind of sandwiches?" Holly interjects. "I need to know the details."

"Cheese and peanut butter. Oddly, that was her favorite."

"You fed cheese and peanut butter sandwiches to a three-year-old? That has to be child abuse."

The mood is lighter now. I laugh, "I'm sure we had fruit juice and Cheerios for you."

The canoe is drifting sideways. We paddle briefly to keep it lined up with the current. Then rest our paddles and drift.

I go on. "There was a lot of activity in the park that day. People were out because it was the weekend, and we had just come through a rainy spell. The smell of fresh rain still lingered beneath the trees. We found a spot on a hill and looked down on everything that was going on around us. And looking out the other way we could see the river twisting towards the bay. There were sailboats tacking about like little bathtub toys."

Holly turns back to me. "I remember that day," she exclaims. "But in my version, there's a kite. A little boy with a kite."

I pause. "I had forgotten. But you're right. It was a little freckle-faced kid, maybe a year older than yourself. He was struggling mightily to get his kite in the air. Back then, there were no fancy dragon or parachute kites. It was just two sticks and a triangle. We watched him for maybe ten minutes. He started running, letting out the kite string, but he just couldn't run fast enough to get it up in the air. Without warning, your mom jumped up and ran down the hill to help him. She held the kite high in the air while he let out twenty-five yards of string. Then your mom shouted, 'Go,' and he took off running as fast as his little feet could. It was touch and go for a few seconds, but the kite started rising, fifty feet, a hundred feet, two hundred feet. The kid had a grin on him a mile wide. Your mom gave him a thumbs up and headed back up to our picnic blanket. Your mom was like that. She'd surprise you with a random act of kindness when you least expected it."

There's an unusually large wave from a passing motorboat. Instinctively, we paddle into the wave, in silence, until the wake from the motorboat dies down.

"It's funny," Holly says. "Now that I think about it, I'm pretty sure I was the kid with the kite."

"Don't think so. I'm pretty sure you were off pouting because your mom was playing with another kid."

But Holly is unconvinced. "It had to be me. I remember the sunlight filtering through the kite as it sailed up on a breeze. It was a heavenly glow, almost like an angel's halo. Everyone in the park was watching."

For a moment, I wonder if Holly really was the kid with the kite. If maybe I just got the moment all jumbled up in my head. "Maybe you're right," I finally say. "It was so long ago."

We paddle further out into the mainstream. The river is surprisingly swift. As we paddle, I try to separate the little girl that I raised from the grown-up woman that's hated me for so long.

"What happened?" Holly asks.

"What do you mean?"

"Why didn't it work out with you and my mom?"

"She always wanted more," I try to explain.

"More of what?"

"Everything. Money. Travel. Things."

"You've told me that before," Holly says. "I don't buy it. It's such a convenient explanation. It's all her fault."

"No. No. Not at all. But I was just happy with the postage stamp yard and the little girl with the cute dimples."

The current is even swifter now. I've always been a good swimmer and have been around water all my life, but there's something about the power of flowing water that makes me ill at ease.

Holly senses my concern and tells me not to worry. "The river is swollen from the recent rain," she says. "This is nothing. You should see the rapids below Great Falls. Ian had a friend who capsized and got stuck in a hydraulic."

"Hydraulic?"

"A hole in the river where the current swirls around like water in a washing machine."

"What happened to him?"

"When the hydraulic finally spit him out, he was barely alive."

"That's horrific."

We drift along in silence. Then Holly says, "That homeless man the other night, you know him?"

"Not really. He's just someone I bumped into one night when I couldn't sleep. He's harmless."

"I'm not so sure," Holly says. "He was ranting about a plot to assassinate Gorbachev. He could be seriously deranged."

"He's just mostly looking for cigarette money."

Holly turns to me and points to shore. Ian's waving to us. "This is our stop," Holly says as we begin to paddle in.

Soon, we are gliding through shallow water to the shore. Ian wades out and pulls us onto the beach. "How was it?" he asks.

"Okay," Holly says.

"It's a beautiful day for it," I say and introduce myself to Ian.

"You're not the monster I was expecting," he jokes.

Holly jabs him in the arm, giving him an ugly look. But I have to laugh. There's something refreshing about Ian's honesty.

The three of us wrestle the canoe into the back of Ian's pickup truck and tie it down.

"Maybe we can do it again sometime," I suggest.

"Maybe," says Holly.

All three of us squeeze into the cab of the truck with Holly in the middle. The pickup's worn springs make for a bumpy ride. It's been years since I've been this close to Holly. I try to see the grown woman sitting beside me, but all I can see is a little girl with a skinned knee and a wrecked bicycle.

Holly asks Ian about something that happened at work, at the Library of Congress. "Do you remember that memo from Jimmy Carter?" she says.

"You mean the research director's crazy memo. The one that mentioned Jimmy Carter's odd interest in UFOs, and, almost as an afterthought, a CIA plot to assassinate a central committee member."

"That's the one."

"What about it?"

"Nothing. It's just such an odd thing. I can't get it out of my mind."

WRAP UP

I SQUIRM IN MY SEAT at the conference table. It's an involuntary reflex. Donna nudges me to stop. I'm being disruptive. I stop the squirming but continue to tap my foot under the table. Kloucek is briefing the optimization module to Markowitz. The room is full of bureaucrats, including the secretary's deputies that were invited by Markowitz. "It's the decision-making tool we need," he tells Markowitz. "Remember our motto: Let's be great together. This will be the primary tool we use to make those decisions."

It's all very well received by Markowitz. And also by the secretary's deputies. Markowitz is nodding his head up and down in approval. Nodding his head up and down to the deputies as if to say: *See, this is the tool we've needed all along. This will legitimize everything we've been working toward. This is the path forward.*

Except it's all mine. The presentation, the notes, the talking points. And Donna's. She knew exactly what spin to give everything for Markowitz and the secretary's deputies.

Kloucek goes on, "The software developers," a nod in my direction, "didn't think it was possible within the original time frame, but we insisted because without it, we have no decision tool. Again, let's be great together."

"Exactly," Markowitz responds, his head nodding up and down.

My foot is now tapping like crazy under the table. It's too much. Kloucek's the one. I want to shout. He's the one who put the monkey wrench in the optimization module. Not us. Instead, I look at Donna, rolling my eyes. She gives me a faint smile, as if to say, *there's nothing that can be done; Kloucek's completely out of control.*

But in the middle of this little exchange, I realize that Cronin has quietly slipped into the conference room and is now sitting by the window, tapping his fingers on the glass. Does he even know where he is?

Out of the blue Cronin says, "Commie bastards." He's looking out the window, to a point in the far distance.

"Pardon me?" Kloucek says, looking at Cronin. But Cronin pays no attention and continues looking out the window. Markowitz now realizes we've deviated from the presentation and is looking to Kloucek for an explanation.

Donna steps in. "Michael and Jonathan," she says, "need to be thanked for getting the requirements for the optimization module fleshed out so quickly."

"Yeah, thanks," Kloucek says. "Let's just hope they can get the software completed on time."

The implication by Kloucek that we are behind the curve, not leaning forward in the foxhole, is the last straw. I'm about to speak up and point out that it was Kloucek that was not leaning forward in the foxhole, when Donna grabs my forearm and squeezes tightly. My cue that now is not that moment to speak up.

But then Markowitz says just that. He says, "Usually you guys have all sorts of ideas on how we can spend our money, but it doesn't sound like you were leaning forward in the foxhole on this one."

With that Markowitz shuffles his papers together, pushes himself from the table, and gets up. The secretary's deputies shuffle their papers together and get up. Kloucek gets up and clears his throat. "Good meeting," he says. He points his finger at me like a gun. He pretends to pull the trigger. He makes a clicking sound.

Kloucek and Markowitz walk out of the conference room together, Kloucek going on and on about all of the features of the optimization module. Kloucek says something funny, and Markowitz laughs and slaps him on the back. I'm certain it is at my expense.

Cronin gets up, stretches his arms, scratches his belly. "Optimize this," he says and deliberately knocks over a chair. I'm stunned. Not by Cronin kicking the chair, but by the idea that on some level, Cronin was aware of what was going on in the room. As Cronin slips out of the room, he looks at me as if he's never seen me before. The way a person might look at a stranger he's found in his kitchen in the middle of the night.

Donna and I are left alone in the conference room. "Sorry about pinching your arm," she says, "but I could tell you were about to correct Kloucek."

"Sorry. But he's got it coming."

"I know, but we need to focus on the big picture."

"Okay."

"By the way," she says, "the office picnic is this weekend. You're invited. Will you be around? The hot dogs and potato chips are on Uncle Sam, but you have to bring your own beverage."

"You mean beer?"

"Actually. I had you figured for a red wine guy."

"That's an insult," I joke.

"So, are you coming?"

"Only if you're going to be there. I don't want to have to make small talk with Kloucek."

"I have to be there. Kloucek put me in charge of decorating the picnic shelter."

"Can I help?"

"Just show up and provide some moral support."

"Okay. Where is it?"

"It's always at the same place. Great Falls."

"How about Cronin? Does he come to these things?"

"It's odd. Everyone makes a point not to say anything about it when he's around. Yet he somehow has a way of finding out."

COLD WAR 3

A LONE BIG-EARED BAT CLINGS atop one of the tallest Crystal City office buildings, looking down on the pedestrian bridge to the airport. In its pursuit of tiger moths and June bugs, it has made its way from the hills upriver, from its roost in the crumbling chimney of an abandoned warehouse. Hunting has been good, and the big-eared bat has earned a brief rest. But back in the chimney of the abandoned warehouse, a pup waits impatiently for its feeding. There's more hunting to be done. The bat launches itself into the air, descending in a long, lazy spiral, plucking unsuspecting insects from the air, until it alights on the rail of the pedestrian bridge. The hardened TV is still tuned to the same channel. Coincidently, the same BBC history show is on. This time the focus is on the rise and fall of Mikhail Gorbachev.

The dry, nasal intonations of the BBC announcer drone on, "In America, President Ronald Reagan is usually given credit for the fall of the Iron Curtain. In this version of the history of the Cold War, the Strategic Defense Initiative and other US defense programs are credited with breaking the military will of the Russians. The relentless military spending of the US drove Gorbachev to throw in the towel and implement Western-style economic and political reforms, ending in the fall of the Berlin Wall. However, more thoughtful analysts, including your narrator, attribute the fall to the forces of reformation set in motion by the Russian premier,

Mikhail Gorbachev. Reforms made necessary by the inefficiency and corruption of the communist system."

There's a pause in the narration as old footage of Russian tractors plowing wheat fields comes on. Unlike their sleek Western counterparts, these tractors are very pedestrian and utilitarian in design. Then come scenes of Russian farm workers with pitchforks, poking at bales of hay. Occasionally, one of them smiles into the camera as if to say: *See, despite the propaganda in your capitalist press, things aren't so bad.*

The narrator continues, "And how did this young upstart, Mikhail Gorbachev, become the youngest leader of Russia since Vasily Lenin? A bright student, he studied law at Moscow University and agricultural economics at the Agricultural Institute, training that served him well as he rose rapidly through the ranks of the Communist Party to first secretary for agriculture and a member of the central committee. In 1979, he was appointed to the Politburo and led Andropov's reform of the leadership of the party, replacing ministers and regional directors with those with more Stalinist leanings. At the death of Chernenko, Mikhail Gorbachev was selected as first secretary of the communist Party. He was astoundingly young at fifty-four. Why Gorbachev? Why not any one of the other bright, talented young party members? There's no adequate answer for this. Some say it was just a case of being in the right place at the right time, catching the eye of Andropov, who became his mentor. Others say he had a secret weapon in his wife, Raisa Gorbacheva. His intellectual equal and perhaps the force that drove him to climb the ranks of the Communist Party."

More newsreel footage fills the screen. There are missiles being towed through Red Square, all sleek and silvery with big red stars on the nose cone. Communist dignitaries sit in a grandstand atop the Kremlin and solemnly observe the procession. Then scenes from an American missile silo in South Dakota cut in. Airmen are preparing to launch an ICBM missile, not knowing if it's just a drill or the real thing.

The big-eared bat flutters over to cling to the cage of the hardened TV, mistaking the flickering images of the Cold War as possible prey.

It pauses, confused by the image of Raisa Gorbacheva in Reykjavik, Iceland, posing for reporters. It's time to return to her pup for a feeding, but she lingers on the faint hope that the images on the hardened TV may still prove to be edible.

The BBC narrator continues, "Raisa Gorbacheva is an interesting person in her own right. She was often criticized by her husband's political enemies for her flamboyant style and dress, but her bright countenance and cheerful personality was quite a political asset for her husband, charming such desperate international figures as Fidel Castro and Margaret Thatcher."

The narrator continues. This time, his voice drips with irony, "Did the policies of the Reagan administration cause the communist regime to implode in its attempt to keep up with the military spending of the West? Does any serious Cold War scholar still believe this myth? Long before rising to the head of the Communist Party, Gorbachev had begun to make his mark as a reformer. With Andropov's blessing, he replaced ministers and regional directors that were not making sufficient progress towards their industrial and agricultural quotas. The Communist Party had grown stagnant, with little incentive for individual ministers to meet industrial growth quotas. As first secretary, Gorbachev implemented his policies of *glasnost, perestroika*, and *uskorenie*. That is, more press and personal freedom, more privatization of production, and an acceleration of economic growth. These internal reforms, plus withdrawing from Afghanistan and reversal of the Brezhnev Doctrine, set into motion forces of democratization that not only undermined the power of the Communist Party but eventually Gorbachev himself. Leading to his house arrest and the rise of Boris Yeltsin.

"As an odd footnote to the rise and fall of Gorbachev, recently declassified CIA documents suggest that black-funded agencies within the CIA—black-funded meaning they were elements within the CIA that were outside of congressional control—had an odd distrust of Gorbachev from the moment he was identified as a likely successor to

Andropov. Evidently fearful that his reform tendencies could tip the delicate scales of the Cold War and undermine the CIA's authority in the West. That a reformer would upset the status quo of détente, either the Russian empire would go tumbling out of control, or there would be more friendly political relations with the West.

"These black-funded operatives did not like either result. These documents go so far as to suggest that while he was a member of the Politburo and long before he had risen to first secretary, black-funded operatives within the CIA had seriously considered an assassination of Gorbachev to eliminate him as a possible successor to the position of first secretary."

The big-eared bat cocks its head as the narrator signs off and white noise fills the screen of the hardened TV. There's a fleeting thought of the pup back in the chimney of the abandoned warehouse, ready for its feeding, aggravated over the delay. The bat flits about and spreads its wings, still unsure whether the flickering shadows and images of the hardened TV can be hunted down and eaten.

There's the hollow echo of random gunfire. The hardened TV explodes, sending glass shards flying in all directions. The big-eared bat is knocked back off the rail, beating its wings disparately to remain airborne. Then, in fits and starts, it gains altitude and beats a course to the chimney of the abandoned warehouse and its hungry pup.

OFFICE PICNIC

It's the Saturday morning of the office picnic. I'm standing in the lobby of the hotel with a small cooler of beer hanging awkwardly from my arm. I volunteered again to help Donna with the preparations. She told me she couldn't put me through that. A lot of blowing up of balloons and hanging up of plastic bunting. "You'd be exhausted by noon," she told me. "Men don't have the constitution for decorating."

Standing in the lobby, I think of Holly. Wondering if maybe by trying to save the memory of her mom, I sent us down an even worse path. Maybe it's like Jimmy says: the truth is always better than the lie. By trying to fabricate a future in which Holly's mom didn't get drunk and wrap our car around a tree, I fabricated a future in which an innocent little girl never knew her mother and grew to hate her father. "A little girl needs a mom," I think out loud. "Not some old coot feeling sorry for himself all the time."

But this is not a day for beating myself up. It's a day for drinking beer, maybe flirting with Donna. A day for forgetting the past. I march boldly out the front of the hotel. There are two cabs with each cabbie sitting in the driver's seat casually reading a newspaper. I lean into the window of the first cab. "Great Falls?" I ask.

"Sure. Jump in," says the cabbie as he folds up his newspaper.

"No rush," I tell him, throwing the cooler in the back seat and sliding in. I'm counting on getting a ride back from the picnic with Donna.

The cabbie makes small talk as we zip in and out of Beltway traffic. He goes on about politics and the poor state of the world, and how no one gives a damn anymore. Then he says, "You know, I don't get too many fares to Great Falls. There's something about that place that spooks people out."

"What do you mean?"

"Lots of drownings. Last time, it was a family picnicking on the rocks. Anyone could tell you that's a bad idea. Little girl got too far out on the rocks and was swept away. You a photographer? Seems like the only fares I get to go out there are photographers."

"Nope."

"Just sightseeing?"

"Office picnic."

"Weird place for an office picnic."

"Don't know. Never been there."

"Anybody can just walk out on the rocks. No fence. No barriers. Wouldn't let my kids go there. No sir. Too dangerous."

"I'll stay off the rocks. Promise."

"Do what you want. But I'm just saying I would never take my kids there."

By now we've exited the Beltway, driving down the two-lane road that runs parallel to the river. Visible through the trees is a thundering, shimmering snake of silver. I feel the presence of the river in my bones.

We pull into the parking lot near the picnic area. I pay the cabbie and grab the cooler of beer. "Stay away from the rocks," the cabbie shouts as I head up to the picnic area. But he's laughing, and it weirds me out.

I track down Donna at the picnic shelter. "Hi," I say. "I brought beer."

Donna says, "Great. Except Markowitz frowns on alcohol at these things."

"A picnic without beer? Isn't that un-American?"

She smiles. "Actually, I need a beer. I've been doing all the work, and Kloucek's been taking all the credit."

"What a guy."

She hands me a box full of little American flags wedged into blocks of wood. "Could you put one of these on each table?"

"Sure." I start to make my way from table to table. I see Kloucek talking to one of Donna's coworkers. "Hi," I say.

"What are you doing here?" Kloucek asks. "I didn't realize contractors were invited."

"Just here to observe my tax dollars at work," I tell him. Kloucek gives me a quizzical look and returns to his conversation.

I'm at the last picnic table in the rear. I straddle the bench and place the last American flag in the middle. Donna comes over and sits down across from me.

"The food table is not officially open yet," she tells me. "But I grabbed some corn chips to tide us over. I'm so glad you could make it."

"Thanks for inviting me. When do we get to eat?"

She laughs. "Kloucek usually makes a few feel-good comments, then it's a mad dash to the serving table."

I nibble the chips. In the background, there's the roar of the falls. The cabbie's right, I think. This is a weird place to have a picnic. I notice that there are only a handful of kids about. I count them to myself for later reference. Six. I watch Donna nibbling on some chips. She seems preoccupied with all the picnic goings-on. I begin to wonder if maybe it's a mistake. Donna's too busy. I'm feeling uncomfortable. The weirdness. The falls. It's awkward with Donna.

Kloucek makes his way to the front of the shelter. He clears his throat and makes a quick speech about what a successful year it's been, how none of it would have happened without this great bunch of guys and gals. I fiddle with the plastic ware and smile at Donna. Her hair is shimmering from the brilliant sunlight that seems to penetrate even the shadows of the picnic shelter. Kloucek closes with, "Remember, let's be great together."

I resist the urge to reach over and touch Donna's hair. "Can we eat now?" I joke instead.

"Not until old Woolsey blesses the food."

"Who's old Woolsey?"

"He's that gentleman with the foot-long beard?" she says, pointing across the shelter.

"Are you sure he's alive? His eyes are shut, and he hasn't moved since I got here."

"He's never let us down. I'm betting on him."

I smile some more. But maybe because of the bright sunlight, it's Helen smiling back at me. It's all in slow motion. Her hair is tossing wildly. There are dark woods all around. Her smile turns into a manic laugh.

A voice interrupts my trance. It's Donna. "Oh my God," she says. Her hand grips my arm.

"What's wrong?" I ask, as the image of Helen fades from my mind.

Donna's pointing across the picnic shelter to a lone staggering figure. It's Cronin, I realize with a start.

"He's drunk!" Donna whispers in horror.

Cronin makes his way to the PA system at the front of the shelter. He clears his throat and grabs the microphone, which is still live from Kloucek's speech. "Fucking commie bastards," he shouts. There's embarrassed silence. A gust of wind sweeps through the picnic shelter. Kloucek gets up to take the microphone from him. Cronin just pushes him aside and continues to rant. "Fucking Jimmy Carter," he says. "Screwed up the whole damn thing." Then Cronin throws the microphone aside and stumbles off into the nearby woods.

Everyone sits in stony silence, like time has completely stopped.

"He's completely demented," I finally say.

Donna nods in agreement.

In the background, the roar of the falls has become even louder.

BEN AGAIN

BEN LURKS IN THE SHADOWS of Michael's hotel. Looking for half-smoked cigarettes, he tells himself. But the truth is he's been obsessed with Michael ever since he witnessed the scene in Luna with Blue Ties. Thinking that somehow Michael will lead him to Blue Ties. "Where are we off to this morning?" Ben asks, watching Michael drive off in the cab.

Approaching the other cab in front of the hotel, he jumps into the back seat before the startled driver can say anything. "Follow that guy," he tells the cabbie.

"You've got to be kidding," the cabbie tells him. "I ain't taking you nowhere. Get the hell out of my cab, you're stinking it up."

Ben reaches deep down into his clothing. The cabbie thinks he's about to pull a knife. That he's being robbed. But Ben pulls out a fifty-dollar bill. "How about this?" he says.

"That's a start."

"Thanks, pal," Ben says and slaps the cabbie on the back. "Follow that guy."

"You mean that guy that just got in the other cab?"

"Yeah."

"Sure, pal."

But now Ben's sad. It's taken years to parlay the few coins he's found here and there into fifty dollars. The fifty dollars he was saving just in case he ever met up with Shannon again so he could at least buy her dinner. Now he wonders if he's wasted the fifty dollars. If maybe Michael's just headed downtown to do some sightseeing. If maybe the guy in Luna wasn't Michael at all, but just a guy that looked like Michael. *Everyone has a double*, he thinks, nodding his head.

He can tell now that they are headed out beyond the suburbs. They exit the Beltway and head down a two-lane road. Ben has the sudden realization that he is now out in the woods. "The open air," he whispers to himself. It's been years since he last left the shadows of the bridges and buildings of Crystal City. He rolls down the window in the back of the cab and lets the fresh suburban air roll in. He takes a deep breath; he hears the sound of a raging river.

"Hey, buddy, what you doing?" the cabbie yells over his shoulder. "You're making me nervous."

Ben wants to smack the cabbie on the back of his head. Instead, he rolls up the window. "Sorry," he says. He senses that things are afoot, that things are going to happen soon. And he doesn't want to disrupt the flow of events that are about to unfold.

They speed through the silver light filtering through the woods. His spirits soar as a gust of wind sends dead leaves swirling about the speeding cab. He takes this moment, while the cabbie is focused on making his way through the swirling debris, to roll down the window again. The cool air again rushes in. He can taste the decaying woods on his lips.

"What'd I tell you?" the cabbie shouts over his shoulders. "Roll up the fucking window."

But now Ben is feeling like the old Ben, the Ben of thirty years ago. *I was the king of the world*, he thinks. *I could have done anything, if it wasn't for that fucking Blue Ties.*

He leans across the front seat and whispers in the cabbie's ear. "Screw you. You got your fifty bucks."

The cabbie starts to say something but thinks better of it. Now he just wants to dump this guy and get back to the more predictable confines of the city. Nothing good happens when you come out here.

They pass a sign that says Great Falls State Park. Up ahead the cab they have been following pulls into a gravel parking lot and comes to a stop.

"This is good enough," Ben says. "Stop here."

Even before the cab rolls to a stop, Ben swings the door open and lunges out. He stumbles, rolls to the ground, but is quickly on his feet again.

"What about my tip," the cabbie shouts after him.

Ben dashes into the woods and makes his way along a narrow trail, instinctively going towards the sound of the rushing falls.

He climbs a large rock on a ledge, looks down into the falls, and sits. He grabs his knees and begins to rock back and forth. The rush of the water is deafening, but that's not what Ben hears. He hears voices from his past—the voices of his mom, of Shannon, of Blue Ties.

The moment is here, he whispers to himself. He strokes his purple scarf, Shannon's scarf.

He sings softly to himself:
> *Shannon, will you love me;*
> *Shannon, will you leave me;*
> *Shannon, will you break my heart?*

Then he sings another tune:
> *Blue Ties in the closet;*
> *Blue Ties in the hall;*
> *It's time, Blue Ties,*
> *To take a little fall.*

IAN'S CLUE

ALL IS QUIET in the Library of Congress except for the beating of small wings. A sparrow is still trapped inside, living in the shadows, only coming out when all the tourists and employees have left. It flits high overhead, following Ian as he makes his way down the Great Hall to the Main Reading Room. Ian throws his backpack on the nearest table.

Outside, it's going to be a warm day, but inside, the AC has been going all night. Ian grumbles to himself. But this has happened before, and he's prepared. He puts on a sweatshirt that he pulls from his backpack. His plan is to finish up cataloging the box of letters and memos from Jimmy Carter before the library opens up to the public. Then maybe take a stroll about the mall, maybe visit the new Smithsonian exhibit on ancient South American textiles.

Ian goes to retrieve the box of letters and memos from the rear of the book stacks. It's not there. He figures Holly must have moved it and gives her a call at home.

"Where's the box of stuff we were going through the other day?" he asks her.

"I probably put it in the boiler room," she says.

"Why did you do that?"

"I wanted it out of the way until we finished cataloging it and couldn't think of anyplace else."

Then she adds, "What in the world are you doing working on a Saturday morning?"

"I'm not really sure, but the lack of any kind of social life must have something to do with it. You seeing your dad today?"

"I'm changing the oil in my car, like it's any of your business."

"Sorry."

"Besides, I think he said something about going to an office picnic today."

"Okay. See you Monday."

"Bye."

"Bye."

Ian makes his way to the document storing room. He rustles about in the corner but can't find the carton with the Carter papers. He sifts through some old paint cans, a bottle of vodka. He picks the vodka up and examines it in the weak light from an overhead window. "Good stuff," he says to himself. The director's stash? He sifts through some more stuff: an old brittle pair of boots that had last seen some action in some long-forgotten battle, an old musket. *Could have been Paul Revere's*, he thinks, *just laying here like junk in someone's attic.*

He sees a carton tucked beneath an old drop cloth and pulls it out. He hauls it back to the table in the main reading room. He sits down, blows the dust off. Everything is quiet. Ian has the feeling that there's something amiss. He looks about, seeing the shadow of the sparrow as it dashes from ledge to ledge. He tries to relax. Pulls odds and ends from the box. There are some political buttons going back to Woodrow Wilson, a bayonet with a Nazi insignia.

Then he pulls out a pile of letters tied together with a string. He takes one out and reads it. It's from the same director of research that had responded to Jimmy Carter's request for permission to view the extraterrestrial collection at the Vatican Library. This letter is dated several years later. It is a warning about a plot to assassinate Gorbachev. With great agitation Ian reads on. It is a plot by a secret US government agency that has been in the works for many years.

He starts pulling letters from the pile at random, quickly scanning them and then throwing them aside. Finally, he comes across a more strident letter that discusses the plot in detail. It's to take place in Luzhniki Stadium during the Moscow Olympics. That in fact it's an unauthorized plot that the CIA is trying to uncover. Being led by a rogue agent with a long history of participating in CIA black-funded projects, early mind control experiments, smuggling drugs from South America. A special activities agent, schooled in assassination, he's completely ruthless and goes by the code name Blue Ties.

Ian mulls over this last detail. *Blue Ties, that has a familiar ring to it*, he thinks. Slowly but deliberately his mind makes its way back to the truck ride back from the river with Holly and Michael. *That's it*, he thinks. Holly's story about the homeless man she ran into in the underground mall, Michael's paranoid friend. He was ranting about some insane plot and his hatred for a Mr. Blue Ties.

He calls Holly back. "How's the oil change going?" he asks.

"Piece of cake," she says.

"Don't suppose I can get you to change the oil in my Civic? I'll pay."

She ignores this last comment. "What do you want?" she asks.

"Right. You're dad's buddy, the homeless guy—"

"The lunatic."

"Turns out . . . Not so crazy. There really is a Blue Ties. Sounds like a nasty character. Unauthorized assassinations. All that messy stuff."

"How do you know this?"

"Letters. I found some old letters from the Carter years. Actually mentions a CIA rogue agent named Blue Ties."

"I'm sure it's just coincidental," Holly says. "Besides, the homeless guy was ranting about some insane plot to assassinate Gorbachev at the Moscow Olympics. How crazy is that?"

"According to this letter, not so crazy."

"What do you mean?"

"That's the plot. Blue Ties, the Moscow Olympics, and Gorbachev."

"You're making that up."

"No. Honest. It's the plot in the letter."

"I swear, if you're making this up, I'll get even."

"You know me better than that."

"I know you like to have fun at my expense, that's what I know."

Ian laughs nervously into the phone. Runs his finger along the crease of the letter. "You know, this letter gives me the creeps. I think we ought to tell your dad. Warn him about this homeless guy."

"You're joking. That was all years ago. Surely, you don't think there's any danger now?"

"Probably not. But I get the feeling there's some kind of unfinished business out there. That this isn't finished yet. The karmic cycle isn't complete. Where's your dad?"

"Have you lost your marbles? Karmic cycle? Really?"

"Where's your dad?"

"I'm not sure. I think he was going to a picnic."

"A picnic?"

"His company's doing work for some government agency. They invited him to their annual picnic."

"And he went? Those things are no fun."

"I think he's got a lady friend. Occasionally he mentions someone named Donna."

"Where's the picnic?"

"Great Falls."

"What? That's not a very good place for a picnic. People have been known to slip off the rocks and get swept away to their deaths."

There's silence on the other end. Ian senses that Holly's grown frustrated with him. It's just weird. The homeless guy talks about hating this guy named Blue Ties. There's this rogue CIA agent that no one knows what happened to named Blue Ties.

"Look," he finally says. "I'm going to pick you up in twenty minutes. We're going to an office picnic."

"You're kidding."

"Nope. Look, you're done changing your oil. I'm tired of working in this tomb. Let's get out. Go to Great Falls. If we see your dad, we just might mention that his crazy homeless friend isn't so crazy."

"That's ridiculous. Besides, I've had enough daddy time for a while."

"I'm going, with or without you. In fact, my backpack is on, and I'm headed out."

"Alright," Holly sighs. "But you are really being ridiculous about this."

CONFRONTATION

THE PICNIC IS WINDING DOWN. Donna is off collecting the miniature flags and placing them in a cardboard box for next year's picnic. I get up from the table and find a path going off into the woods. The sound of the falls grows louder the further down the path I go. I'm alone in the woods. I fantasize that I'm the last man standing, post-holocaust. It's just the rocks, the water, and me. No credit cards, no mortgage, a clean slate. Maybe Donna survived, and Holly, and maybe her friend, Ian. I wind my way through some house-size rocks. I have the odd thought that maybe Helen's spirit is out here somewhere among the rocks and trees.

I make my way to a cliff overlooking the falls. There's been a recent rain, so there is a thunderous flow over the falls. I inch my way out to the edge and look down. It's at least fifty feet down to the torrent of the falls. I can't believe that people bring their kids here. Some yards away a lady and her daughter I saw across the table at the picnic are peering down into the chasm. I want to warn them of the danger. Surely, they understand that one misstep and it's all over.

I follow a slender trail along the cliff away from the woman and her daughter. If the worst happens, I don't want to be a witness. I slash through some scrub brush, and then before me lies a vista of the river as far as the eye can see. There's not a stretch of smooth water. It's all riffles and eddies and whirlpools and huge rocks that seem to have just fallen out of the sky. It's late in the day, and it all takes on a faraway, faded hue. I'm transfixed at the sight, lost in time. For a moment I have no understanding of why I'm here. The steps that brought me here, the cab ride, the picnic with Donna. It's all a blank.

A twig snaps, and I'm immediately alert. At a very basic level I feel threatened even though my mind tells me that it's probably just some kid from the picnic. I turn to shoo the kid away from the cliffs. But it's Cronin. He's smoking a large cigar and has an odd, twisted smile on his face. He's wearing his blue tie.

"Boo," he says. "Don't slip." Then he laughs. It's a creepy, machine-gun kind of laugh. Rapid and relentless. "Don't you just love a good picnic?" he goes on. "Wieners. Free beer. Pretty girls." He says this poking his cigar in my face.

I have to take a step back. Slipping momentarily on some loose rocks, I find myself staring into the belly of the falls. I regain my balance.

"Something I've been meaning to ask you," I say to Cronin. "What exactly is your job?"

"To protect little shits like you from the commies."

"You didn't get the memo? The Cold War is over. We won."

Cronin takes a long draw from his cigar. A change comes across his face. "Fucking Carter," he says, like now we're best friends. "He ruined the whole damn thing. There was a balance. A natural order of things. A balance of opposing forces. We knew Gorby was a reformer. Someone who could screw up the whole natural order of things. Reformers always screw things up."

It sounds crazy, but now I'm starting to connect the dots. Gorbachev. Cronin. It has a familiar ring to it. I think maybe it's time to get back with Donna. Being stuck on a lonely ledge overlooking a massive waterfall, with Cronin between me and solid land, leaves me feeling uneasy.

Then things get even crazier. Ben steps out of the bushes. "Remember me, Blue Ties?" he asks. "Where's that sick buddy of yours? Dr. Sewell?" Then he looks at me and shakes his head sadly. "I thought we were friends? I should have known better."

"I don't know what you're talking about," I tell Ben.

"I saw you two, talking in the restaurant. You're one of his minions."

"That was just a chance encounter," I tell him.

"Don't believe you."

I look at Ben. Then look at Cronin. I have the feeling I'm in the presence of forces beyond my control. That this moment was predestined. That's when the final tumblers click into place. Cronin is Blue Ties. Blue Ties is Cronin. There really was a plot to assassinate Gorbachev? Incredible.

"How did you get here?" I ask Ben. It's the only thing I can think of to say.

"Never mind that," Ben says.

A look of wonder crosses Cronin's face. "Jesus Christ. It can't be. Ben? Is that you? I thought the outfit had disposed of you long ago. What cave did you crawl out of? You look horrible."

"Screw you. It's your turn. Say your prayers because it's all over for you, Blue Ties." Then, like an enraged bull, Ben rushes Cronin.

But Cronin's still laughing. "This is just too rich. Wait till the boys back at the outfit hear about this."

I've been frozen on one spot during this whole exchange between Cronin and Ben. "Ben, no!" I finally shout and step in front of Ben. But it's too late. Ben's momentum takes all three of us over the ledge.

We fall all splayed out and arms grasping at the empty air. Instinctively, I struggle to twist about and get my feet under me. I look down. Time has stopped. I look about for Ben and Cronin, but the rocks, the water, the tumbling people, all blur together. The inevitable impact with the rushing water of the river sends water gushing up my nose, into my ears, up my ass. I'm immediately swept downstream in the vortex of the falls. Somehow, I get my feet pointing downstream and cover my head with my arms. I'm bouncing off rocks. I know I'm injured but feel no pain. There's a painful bump from behind. I open my eyes and, in the confusion of the tumbling water, watch as Ben is swept by. His arms are crossed, and there's a smile on his face, as if at last he's at peace with the world. Then Ben's gone in the turgid water.

Then I'm outside myself. A neutral observer witnessing his own destruction. I'm talking to Helen. "Is this what it's like? Death? I wish you would've hung around," I tell her. "I think we could have worked things out."

"Don't worry," she tells me. "I don't think you're going to die today."

"How do you know?"

"Just a hunch. Someone will save you. I think I know more about death than you."

Suddenly, there's sunlight everywhere. Far off, I hear children laughing. Lots and lots of children.

"Am I dead?" I ask Helen.

"I told you, you're not going to die today," she answers. "I'm pretty sure Holly and her boyfriend will save you."

"Why did you have to leave us?" I ask.

"I had unresolved issues from a previous life."

"That's not fair," I say. "You left a little girl without a mother. You left me without hope."

"That's the way the cosmic cookie crumbles," she says. "Plus, I might add in my defense that I'm a perfect housewife and mother in my next life. In fact, I actually die donating a kidney to my sister-in-law."

"Sorry," I tell her.

Then I fall into a deep black hole. All is darkness. There is no sound.

SEARCH

IAN SCRAMBLES DOWN the loose rocks and boulders to a small sandy beach downstream from the falls. Higher up Holly is picking her way down much more carefully. Even though the rapids are much tamer in this stretch of the river the air is still chill from the mist.

There's still a chance they survived, Holly thinks. Ian's kayaked this part of the river and says the currents and back eddies cause a lot of debris and stuff to wash up on this beach. Maybe they washed up somewhere around here.

Now she stands on the beach with Ian. They look around. They look up the rocky path to the road. "The rescue squad will be here shortly," Ian says. "They'll have some divers just in case."

Holly wrings her hands. She grabs Ian by both shoulders and shakes him. "I hate myself," she tells him. "I should have buried the hatchet a long time ago. Now I'll never have a chance. I mean, I hate him for his lies, but he's the only father I have."

Ian takes Holly's wrists. He looks her in the eyes. "I've seen people survive a lot worse. Remember my friend? He got caught in a hydraulic for five minutes. We all thought he was a goner. When he finally popped out, he was still alive, unconscious, but we were able to revive him."

"Tell me again what you saw on the ledge."

"I was like one second too late. Just as I came out of the woods onto the ledge, I saw the homeless guy—"

"Ben?

"Yeah Ben, saying to this Blue Ties character that it's his turn, that the shoe's on the other foot, and it's Blue Ties turn to die. Then he goes for him like a football player about to make a tackle. At the last second your dad stepped between them and Ben took them all over the ledge into the gorge. The last thing I heard was this Blue Ties shouting at Ben, as he was falling, telling him he was a dumb fuck, then laughing, a very sick, perverted laugh. It really creeped me out."

Holly frowns, "I can't believe Ben's whole crazy conspiracy about Blue Ties and the plot to assassinate Gorbachev is true. It's too far-fetched."

"But the letter suggested there was something afoot. My theory is these two guys are relics from the Cold War. That Blue Ties was managing Ben, somehow making him do something he didn't want to do. The CIA is notorious for stuff like that. And Ben finally caught up with him and wanted revenge so bad he was willing to risk his life."

As he's saying this, Ian is making his way further out into the river, hopping from rock to rock. Holly follows but much more carefully. "I'm not so sure about this," she says, but Ian can't hear because even here at the sandy landing, where the current is considerably reduced, there's still the din of the river flowing about the boulders and rock gardens.

There's a shout from Ian. "Over here. I found someone over here."

Holly makes her way carefully across the rocks to Ian.

Ian points to a quiet pool down below them. There's a clump of rags wedged between two rocks. "Quick," he says, "We may not have much time." Holly follows as they find a route across the rocks to the pool below. They wade across the pool with water up to their waist. As they get closer, it's obvious that the clump of rags is actually a person's body face down in the water. With great care, Holly and Ian ease the body over. "Doesn't look like your dad," Ian says somberly.

"It's Ben," Holly says.

Ian checks for a pulse or any sign of life. "He's gone. Let's pull him out of the water and let the rescue squad haul him up to the road."

Together, they slide him through the shallow water to a flat rock. Ian gets on top of the rock and pulls while Holly pushes. "This guy is huge," Ian says, still breathing heavily from the effort.

Ben's eyes are wide open. What looks like a grin is spread across his lips. Somehow Shannon's scarf is still wrapped around his neck.

Holly sits on a nearby rock to catch her breath. She notices something still clutched in Ben's hand. "What's this?" she says. She leans over and carefully pries it from Ben's hand. "My God," she says. "It's a piece of Blue Ties' blue tie."

"What?"

"It looks like a piece of a blue tie. It must be Blue Ties' blue tie. Ben, the homeless guy, wasn't completely crazy."

"The whole thing is insane," Ian says. "It's like we turned over a rock and all these weird little bugs started crawling out."

Holly's quiet for a moment. She gives Ian a sideways glance. "Please! Can we search for my dad," she says at last.

"Okay," Ian says and hops across some more rocks that take him further downstream. Holly tries to follow but gives up. She doesn't have Ian's mountain climbing and outdoor skills. She decides to make her way back up the rocks and follows along from higher up. There's still no sign of Michael. The sun is now setting, and the last golden tendrils are weaving themselves through the woods on either side of the gorge. "It's almost like being in church," Holly thinks. "A huge stone and timber cathedral with the rippling and singing of the river as the choir."

She stands still for a moment, arms at her side. "What have I done with my life," she says to herself, tears welling up in her eyes. "I turn my back on the only human being on the planet that I know loves me. Michael lied, but he was just trying to protect me. Someday I was going to forgive him, after I had punished him enough. Now it could be too late."

Holly grows more anxious. If Michael is still alive, the chances of finding him in the impending darkness are even more remote. Holly squints downriver into the sunlight. There's something that catches her eye, something inconsistent with the swirl and flow of the river. She focuses on a spot that Ian's already searched. There's no doubt in her mind now that it's a distinctly human motion, an arm rising out of the shallows of the river. She shouts down frantically at Ian. But Ian is busy scanning the rocks and inlets and can't hear her.

She makes her way down the rocks and struggles to catch up with him. But he's way too far out on the rocks and Holly knows she has no chance of catching up with him. At last, he turns back and looks her way. She waves frantically with both arms and points to the spot. Ian signals he understands and together they converge to the spot that Holly has been pointing at, a small pool cluttered with tree limbs, dead fish, pieces of Styrofoam, other assorted debris. There's an arm slung around one of the large tree limbs. There's movement.

"I must have missed this because of the debris," Ian says in disbelief. They both wade across the pool, clearing away the debris. Ian grabs a piece of driftwood and holds it like a club. Holly gives him an admonishing look. "Could be this Blue Ties guy," he explains. "Not sure I trust him."

RESCUE

I KNOW SOMETHING BAD HAS HAPPENED. Out beyond me somewhere, there's a ring of blue light. I'm not sure if I'm dead or alive, or somewhere in between, like in another dimension. I remember being swept away, feeling helpless in the incredible torrent of the river. A million images going through my mind at once. Too fast to make any sense out of it. Places I've been. The bedroom of the first house I lived in with Helen, before Holly came along. With hand-me-down furniture and old sheets over the windows. A mist-shrouded lake in the mountains where I fished with my dad. Holly's first-grade classroom, full of giggly kids and papier-mâché projects. People I've known. Chief Hagan, my drill instructor in boot camp who really had it out for college guys. Helen, the day I met her, wearing a crazy yellow hat. Mrs. Conners, the widow who lived one block over when I was growing up and liked to leave her shades open. A small girl I once saw on a subway that had huge elfish eyes whose image I've never been able to get out of my head.

I hear voices that seem to be singing. They're beautiful, too beautiful, like they're aliens or something. Like how the smell of cut flowers always makes me uneasy because that's the smell of funerals.

Now I'm sure my time has come. And what do I have to show for it? One disastrous marriage and a dead wife, years of working for a bureaucracy, a daughter that won't speak to me. How the hell do you defend that at the pearly gates?

Now the light is golden sunlight. Now the voices are talking, not singing. Now the voices converge to one voice. I open an eye not sure if the dead can even open their eyes.

I see a face. It's Holly's. "Are we in heaven?" I ask.

I wipe my face. It's wet and muddy.

"You survived a bad accident. But I think you are going to live."

"An accident?"

"You don't remember?"

"All I remember is walking along a trail, and then everything was upside down, and water everywhere. I couldn't escape the water."

I manage to sit up. My breathing is labored. My ribs throb with each breath I take. I taste blood from somewhere. I try to stand, but Holly insists I sit back down. "Not so fast," she tells me. "The rescue squad is on its way."

"Am I that bad off?"

"Worse," says Holly. "You're lucky to be alive."

Things are starting to come back to me now. "Ben was at the picnic," I tell Holly. "I remember thinking, 'What in the world is he doing here?' We were on the ledge overlooking the falls. Ben was arguing with Cronin. Ben and Cronin seemed to know each other from somewhere. Ben kept calling him Blue Ties. He seemed to think Cronin was that Blue Ties character he was always talking about. The one that was involved in some kind of insane plot to assassinate Gorbachev at the 1980 Olympics. Then Cronin was making fun of him, telling him he should have been disposed of a long time ago. Telling him he would always be a piece of shit, if you'll excuse the expression."

"All three of you went over the ledge into the falls," Holly says. "We found Ben's body. There was no sign of Cronin."

"Ben's dead?"

"I'm afraid so."

"It's weird. I hardly knew the guy, but for some reason I felt a connection with him. Like I could have easily ended up like Ben, homeless and alone. That's the way I felt after your mother died. I felt like wandering the earth, homeless and alone."

In the distance, there's the sound of sirens. Holly takes my hand. "We're going to have you checked out at the hospital. Ian's up at the road to flag down the ambulance."

"I'm feeling much better," I tell Holly. "Who's Ian?"

"My coworker. You met him the day we canoed the river."

"Oh, yeah. You're boyfriend."

"He's not my boyfriend. Just a friend."

"He seemed like a nice guy."

"He is. You owe him your life. He's the one who figured it all out. I thought he was crazy, but thank God he insisted on checking it out."

"What did he figure out?"

"You know, the plot to assassinate Gorbachev. Ian found a letter at the library that corroborated Ben's story. I thought he was crazy, but he insisted we come out here and check it out."

"What did the letter say?"

Holly hesitates. "Look, you're really bad off. We need to talk about this later."

We're both silent for a while. "Holly, I'm sorry I lied to you about your mother. I never should have done that."

"Like I said, hospital first, talk later."

When the ambulance arrives, Ian comes down from the road to help out. Ian and a medic get me on a stretcher and, with great effort, up the rocks to the road.

I call Holly over to the stretcher. "I forgot," I tell her. "I'm here with a lady named Donna up at the picnic shelter. I need to let her know I'm okay."

"You've got a girlfriend?" She asks surprised.

"She's just a friend, a co-worker."

"You need to get to the hospital; I'll send Ian to tell her to meet us there."

"Okay."

Holly rides with me in the ambulance. A medic tends to my head wounds and suggests I remain still in case I've broken some ribs. I realize I'm more injured than I thought. Pain oozes from every pore of my being. I feel every bump as the ambulance races to the hospital.

Holly sits along the bench in the back of the ambulance, across from the medic. The medic periodically checks my pulse.

I pull myself up on my elbows. "Holly," I say. She turns. She seems sad. "I saw her," I say.

"Saw who?" Holly says.

"Your mother."

"Please don't do this."

"No. I'm sure it was really her. I mean I know I was being swept downstream. But I could feel her presence. She told me she was okay. Not to worry about her."

Holly closes her eyes. "It was just a hallucination or something," she says.

"Nope. She told me you and Ian would save me."

That's the last thing I remember until I wake up in the hospital.

PARK BENCH

HOLLY IS DROPPING ME OFF at the hotel. My head is still wrapped in a bandage, my ribs still ache every time I inhale. Seemingly random renovations are scattered across the façade of the entrance and front. Several workmen are in the process of sending a bucket of concrete up a small utility elevator. All is quiet except for the construction.

"What in the world are they doing here?" Holly asks.

"Beats me. I only stay here because they serve fresh bagels every morning. They've been working on this place for years."

We sit silently for a few more seconds. "Thanks for the ride," I tell her. And thanks for smuggling in the Chinese food. I'm not sure how much longer I could've handled that hospital food."

"Sure."

I ease out of Holly's small compact car. A sharp pain shoots through my back as I swing my legs out and brace myself to stand. "Bye," I tell her.

"Bye"

My eyes try to adjust to the bright sunlight. I've been in the controlled environment of the hospital for almost a week.

Holly starts the car as I hobble around to the driver's side to say goodbye again. "You look pathetic," She laughs.

"Thanks." I try to smile but even that hurts.

"I'll swing by tomorrow after work to check on you. I'll bring something for dinner."

"That would be great."

Holly pulls off, but I'm not ready to return to the hotel room. On a whim, I make my way across the street to a small park. But this is an urban park and there are no songbirds or woodland creatures, just pigeons and the occasional underfed squirrel. Just the same, it's nice to be outside, even the dirt and grit is a refreshing change from the antiseptic environment of the hospital. I make my way to the one bench in the middle of the park.

There is no one else in the small park. It's mid-afternoon, and all the workers have long since returned to their cubicles, and all the homeless people are still out scavenging.

It's the homeless that have the darkest secrets. It's their secrets that drive them from their loved ones, from the warm embers of hearth and home. Ben's secret was so fantastic, so far-fetched, how could he share that with anyone? An unwilling hitman for the CIA? A discus thrower taking out Gorbachev? That story will get you institutionalized every time. Maybe that's why Ben preferred to be homeless. Somewhere deep inside himself, he knew he had to share his story. And the only place he could do that without ending up in a mental institution was on the street.

The surprise was that there was a woman. I couldn't believe it when Holly told me that a woman showed up to claim Ben's body. A woman named Shannon Lawson. The story in the newspaper said she was briefly engaged to Ben back in college. That she had been a lifelong friend. Had even offered to help Ben get off the street, but he refused. "He was too proud," she told the newspaper reporter. There was nothing about a plot to assassinate Gorbachev. When asked why they never married, Shannon Lawson just said that Ben was too complicated for her. She was a simple farm girl from Wisconsin. Ben was on the track team and was always traveling for that, but he also was always off on secret meetings with a suspicious character that always wore a dark suit and a blue tie. "I think I was afraid he was involved with the Mafia," she told the newspaper reporter.

My mind turns to my brother Jimmy and what he set in motion with Holly. In the end, it worked out alright. At least Holly's talking to me now. Maybe someday she'll forgive me. Forgive me for lying, for being a clueless dad. Then I have this cosmic thought. Everything's related to everything else. Everything goes round comes round, as they say. Jimmy doesn't contact Holly. Holly doesn't bump into Ben, and Holly doesn't tell Ian Ben's story. Ian doesn't put two and two together, and I die from overexposure in the Great Falls gorge.

There is a God. There is meaning to life.

There's a woman's face in the sunlight. It's Donna. She sits down next to me. "What are you laughing at?" she asks.

"The meaning of life," I tell her. "What are you doing here?"

"I was on my way over to the hotel to see how you were doing."

"You left Kloucek unattended? There's no telling what havoc he'll wreak in your absence."

"I told him no treats this afternoon if he misbehaves," Donna says as she touches the sutures on the side of my head. "How are your wounds doing? You look like you've been to hell and back."

"Thanks."

She takes my hand. "It's sexy," she says. Then in the next breath, "I was so worried about you. I knew Cronin would cause trouble when I saw how drunk he was at the picnic. I should have reported him to a park ranger or something. It's all my fault."

I realize that I've never held Donna's hand and that, despite having gone out to lunch together many times, we've seldom been this close. I can smell her perfume, her hair. I want to invite her up to my hotel room but think better of it. Instead, I say, "Actually, I think it was all predestined to happen. My life was at an impasse. I was stuck in the past. With Holly. With memories of her mother. I was around lots of people yet so alone at the same time. That chance encounter with Ben started a chain of events that broke me loose from all of that. It sent me careening down another path. The path that ends with you sitting here with me on this park bench. The path where I get to see my daughter again. In a very real sense, I am reborn thanks to Ben."

"But he almost killed you in that gorge. You were incredibly lucky you survived. Cronin and Ben didn't make it."

"They found Cronin's body?"

"No. But at this point everyone's assuming he's dead."

"I wouldn't be so quick to write that old buzzard off. He survived a lifetime of special ops with the CIA. Until his body washes up somewhere, I'll be checking under my bed."

We both laugh nervously at that. There's a long pause. "By the way," I ask, "how's the optimization module coming along? Did Kloucek and Markowitz finalize the enhancements?" I hate the fact I've had to resort to shop talk to keep up my end of the conversation.

"Are you kidding? They live to debate this kind of minutia. A final decision would spoil all the fun."

There's another long pause. Traffic in the park is starting to pick up, people sneaking out of work early, homeless people returning from an afternoon of scavenging.

"I like working with you," Donna says out of the blue.

I'm suddenly aware that this is more than just an innocent comment from a coworker. Woven between the words is a plea. Let's say goodbye to the ghosts of the past. We've paid our dues to the dead. Our lives are so empty, when they could be so much more. Please, let's give it a shot and see what happens.

At last, I say, "I think this is the part where I ask you out to dinner tonight."

Donna takes my arm and drapes it around her shoulders. "What a wonderful idea. Of course I'll drive since you're all beat up. Let's go to a place with chocolate waffles. I don't care what else is on the menu. I just want chocolate waffles with chocolate syrup for dessert."

Our eyes meet. There's a light in Donna's eyes that I've never seen before. Or maybe it's been there all along, I was just too blind to notice.

"Chocolate waffles? I had you figured for a cheesecake gal."

Then we chat for a long while. Not about anything cosmic. About kids. About trips. About whether we liked big dogs or little dogs. About if we had ever smoked marijuana in college. About what we would do if we won the lottery. About the strange things that Holly and Ian come across at the Library of Congress. About Jimmy Carter's obsession with UFOs.

We chat until office workers start streaming out of their offices. Until men and women with briefcases and overcoats are walking in all directions in the park, so intent on their homeward-bound journeys that they hardly notice us sitting on the park bench. Then the homeless start to gather in the corners of the park out of the way of the office workers. I watch as they trade and barter among themselves for the little treasures and food they've found in their scavenging.

Now, the traffic out on the highway has picked up and cars are honking incessantly. A large jet lands at the airport and the ground shutters as it reverses its engines. And even though the small park is surrounded by tall office buildings and hotels, the fading sunlight somehow manages to weave its way through the canyons and peaks of Crystal City to find Donna and I sitting on the park bench. She smiles at me. I smile back. I wonder where Cronin is sleeping tonight.

The End

www.ingramcontent.com/pod-product-compliance
Lightning Source LLC
LaVergne TN
LVHW092052060526
838201LV00047B/1348